Umbra

DELILAH MOHAN

Warning

Umbra is a gritty reverse harm romance with situations that may be triggering to some readers. It contains violence, sexual situations, death, destruction, blood and other sensitive matter that might not be right for some readers.

CHAPTER
One

THEA

I am a monster.

The shadow that follows and hunts you in the night.

Umbra.

The haunting face of the unknown.

But I see everything as I cloak myself in darkness. I know everything and if I close my eyes tight enough, I feel everything.

My icy fingers reached out in the dark and, like a wisp of the wind, the blade in my hand sliced through skin, carving into the flesh of my mark. He didn't see me coming. They never did. Not when their curious eyes looked right through the shadows. I pulled the dark around my body like a shield from the world. The pressure of the blade registered too late to save him as his mouth opened in shock. All that escaped was a gargle as blood bubbled up his throat and spilled over his lips.

With a jolt, my blade was removed, pulled from his body with a sickening, wet sound.

Unseen, he still tried to reach for me, still tried to grasp and hold on to something or someone in his last seconds before his legs gave way and he hit the ground, fallen onto his knees. One last blink and his body fell to the side, the last gasp of breath leaving him.

I pulled a camera out of my pocket and snapped two photos. One for me, a keepsake of my triumph. The other I tossed on the body. A calling card, a signature, a taunt. Then I turned my back, my feet sloshing through the blood that oozed from the corpse. That's what he was, a corpse. A target. A mark and a notch on my post of accomplishments. But nothing more than that. Nothing more than an income that would keep me fed until the next order came in.

I walked out of the warehouse and away from the monster that had once been so much worse than me. The man. The human. The offender of too many crimes to ever grant him repentance for his sins. I don't discriminate, though. I will slay man or beast equally as long as the price is right, and the offense demanded it. Everyone's life had a price. The man lying on the warehouse floor just so happened to be worth fifty-five thousand. That was enough to get me by until the next job.

I pulled out my cell phone, typed in the number and rose the phone to my ear. When a male voice answered, I didn't wait for a conversation starter. "It's done. I'll expect my transfer by midnight."

I hung up, knowing the transfer would come. No one dared betray me because if they did, they would be next to feel my blade sink into their skin.

I was halfway down the block when the text came. *It's done.*

I shoved my phone into my pocket and pulled the shadows close. My steps on the pavement were silent, cushioned by the darkness and though I passed the occasional being out way past the regulated curfew, their eyes never fell to mine. Sure, they sensed me. Their ears perking up as they strained to figure out just what was out of order, but their mind and eyes never connected that it was the shadows, that lurked in the dead of night, that they should fear the most.

I walked until I reached my building. The six story walk up was silent, the residents all deep in their slumbers. None of them cared to know that the deliverer of death lurked in their halls. And if they had known, they would beg me to take them too. I pulled the shadows tight around me as I slinked into the entrance, shielding me from prying eyes and questions as I walked past the addicts and prostitutes that littered the hallways.

It was four stories up to reach my apartment. Four stories to climb and hope not a single soul noticed me or spoke. They did sometimes. Those on the verge of death, ready for the reaper to take them, saw past the shadows I hide behind, but they never saw it long. Death would come shortly. Relief from the wretched life they had led. Although the deaths of innocents shouldn't make me happy, it did. The suffering of this world was over and weren't they the lucky ones to pass?

Inside of my apartment, I slammed the door. Locking every lock from the top of the frame down to the floorboard. Some might say it was an overkill. I call it playing it safe. When you live to stalk and kill, you understand the importance of safety. Especially when you take the safety and security away from a mark, watching as the fear filled their eyes, as the realization set in that if they just locked that window, chained the door, double checked their crawl space, they might have lived another day.

Might have. But "might have been" was never a guarantee. Though I wasn't willing to risk it. The minute my door was secured, I went into the kitchen, checking the window. Then moved along the wall of the apartment, testing out each lock, making sure there were no tampers, and securing the rooms. When that was finished, I grabbed my stool and pushed open the crawl space. With a flashlight, I looked around. The traps I set up there went untouched. That was a good sign.

I let the door to the crawlspace drop before I jumped off the stool. After tossing the flashlight onto the bed, I went back to the kitchen, threw the fridge open and grabbed a beer. The taste was disgusting, but after shanking a fucker, it seemed like a good decision. A knife wasn't always my weapon of choice. Sometimes I used my hands, chains, or rope, but never guns. Those proved useless on monsters. Those were useless on beings like me. Unless they were filled with specialized ammunition, but that was impossible to find out here.

After downing half the beer, I carried it over to my desk, pushed in the far corner of the room. I had little furniture; I didn't need it. But I allowed myself the pleasure of an adequate workspace so I could do my job efficiently. Reaching below my desk, I wiggled free the vent cover and pulled out an album. It was my past conquests. My trophies. A memoir to my art and accomplishments.

I removed the photo from my pocket, slathered the back with glue and slapped it on the page. I didn't allow myself to stare too long. I was there, I'd remember. Every moment was engrained into my brain. From the second I first laid eyes on him when he entered the space, to the genuine fear that pulsed off him when he realized he was no longer alone. It was sealed in my memory, mine to keep.

With a slam, I closed the album before placing it back into the vent and replacing the cover. Then I turned my attention to the folder I had gotten this morning. The monsters within were of the DNA type and not of the human variety. A challenge, for sure. Monsters, forced upon this earth different, mutated, predisposed to be an outcast, they were harder to kill. But I'd succeed either way. I always did.

Only, this case was different. Three, there were three

marks, one job. Their offense? I flipped through all the pages. Not a single mention of their offense. "It's not here."

I spoke the words out loud, as if someone were here in the room to dispute the fact. No one was. I grabbed my cell phone and hit speed dial one, waiting for the agency to pick up. They answered on the first ring. "Hello?"

"There is no offense." I stated, not caring who answered.

There was a chair squeak and a noise that indicated someone was straightening up, giving me their full attention. "Thea. Hi. What can I do for you?"

"There is no offense." I repeated.

"I understand, unfortunately when the file was passed down the chain of command here at headquarters, it appears the offenses had been lost."

Fucking government. Was that even possible to lose? "I don't do a job without an offense. It's my rule and you know it."

I had a job and fuck if it wasn't secure, there were always bad guys in this world. But I'll be damned if I killed an innocent person, not again at least.

On the other end of the line, there was a throat clearing. "Thea, have we ever steered you wrong?"

Had they? No. Were they capable? Yes. "I expect an updated list of information by this time tomorrow."

"I might need-" he tried to argue. But it was simple information, and I would not wait.

"Tomorrow."

I hung up the phone before allowing myself to flip the last page and stare into the faces of my next marks.

CHAPTER
Two

THEA

Ansel.

Rex.

Warren.

I rolled the names around in my mind. Even dared speaking them out loud to see what they tasted like on my tongue. The taste was... divinity in its unique form. A taste I'd never experienced before.

But I wouldn't get my hopes up that their deaths would taste as sweet. If anything, their deaths would taste bitter and vile, like the creatures they were.

It took twenty-four hours, almost exactly, to get the new files. Twenty-four hours of waiting. Twenty-four hours of staring at the photos of the men in front of me and wondering what they had done so wrong that the United Government wanted, no... needed, them dead. To send their top assassin could be considered overkill in most cases. But this case, in particular, had me curious.

I looked down at the list of men who had fallen to the trio.

The agents who had failed to recover the deaths of the villains. But the list of agents was weak, and I'd never heard of a single name on it. That raised a single red flag that I pushed down to ignore. I trusted my employer. I had every reason to trust them and not a single reason to question their authenticity.

My finger rubbed over the words as I read, my mind memorizing the details. Details that strangely missed so much about the mark. What were their flaws? I assume they had some. Anyone who made it to this side of the government's list had flaws. They were marked as a mutant, a monster like I was. But mutiny was only a problem when you pick evil over the good of the people.

I squinted at the photos harder, just enough to see some green and blue scales that snuck up the neck of Rex. A mutant form of a reptile, maybe? I've seen some of them before. Harmless. Though, if that was the case, he wouldn't be on my kill list.

I allowed myself to reach the bottom, bypassing the information that was all formal and straight, to the updated information of their offense.

I blinked a few times, trying to believe what I was reading. I couldn't put the crime to the faces. It didn't seem to fit. Women and children trafficking? No. How is that even a thing still in this day and age? I'd take them out, head off their operations before they had a chance to do more damage. And I'd do it tonight.

I search my files further, learning that they preferred to do their business in the city's business district on the furthest dock. Freight, but I bet it wasn't freight they were transporting. Women, children, those who were not capable of transporting themselves and keeping themselves safe were what these vile disgusting men preyed on. It was a harsh world. A hard world and so many things had changed and altered from what it once was. Humans? Humanity was a thing of the past, not mixed and mingled with mutant and monsters, things that go bump in the night, man-made creations that went so utterly wrong. DNA held so many secrets and possibilities and it was ruined, altered, completely fucked by scientists who thought they were a divine entity in themselves.

That's how it happened, at least for me.

A shot. A single medical shot to an infant and single mother who didn't know she had an option to say no. And here I am, twenty-eight years later, a monster of the night. A lurker. A ponderer. A soulless black pit. Now though? Mutiny is no longer a choice made by an uneducated parent. Children aren't born with it. Our DNA altered and fucked with so badly that no longer does a human simply exist. They are formed, monitored, protected by all costs as superior, and I am for the movement. I'm for beings no longer suffering the fate that I had without a choice. I'd protect a human. I'd protect a mutant. I'd protect the option to live freely if you were no danger to those around you.

But women and children trafficking. It was high on my list of unacceptable offenses. My mother was taken, abducted right in front of me while I wrapped my body in shadows and hid and I had never seen her again. I'd not let another family fall to the same fate.

The folders slammed shut in front of me, though I didn't even remember doing so, even with my palm pressed flat against the manilla casing. I'd get these fuckers. That was a fucking vow. Even if I nearly got taken out in the process.

I waited until the sun went down before I left my apartment. Slinking around in the dark was always easier when everywhere, the shadows lurked. Each step against the sidewalk was silent as I made my way toward the dock. Each breath I took was muted by the breeze. If you looked down the street, you wouldn't see me. You'd look right past me and the shadows I kept and assume you were alone. I walk side by side in the street's silence, nearly rubbing shoulders with strangers, but no one could feel my touch.

Invisibility.

It was how I lived. Spending each day being unseen.

I entered the gate of the docks through a crack that wasn't fully closed. A dog growled in my direction, sensing me when human and mutant could not. A human voice screamed from the tiny guard station. "Shut the fuck up, mutt. There isn't anything there!"

If only he knew the truth, he would thank the pup.

The ocean swished calmingly in the distance and if I wasn't on a job, if I hadn't come here to kill, I might have taken the time to sit and listen. To absorb the tranquility of the body of water that the humans and mutants hadn't success-fully been able to ruin, at least not yet. My feet traveled over the gravel as I moved, the rubber of my soles absorbing the sound as I stepped lightly, trying not to shift the tiny pebbles under my body.

I reached paved ground, a blessing after stepping over the tiny stones of the dock vehicle entrance. I turned right, heading for the very last building. A warehouse that appeared dark from here, but appearance meant nothing to me. I'd been in darker places, and time and time again I've proven, as I hugged the shadows around me, that I was not afraid of the dark, it was the light that people should fear.

The closer I got, the more stifling the silence became. It was too silent, suspiciously so, that I didn't trust it. My hands fell to my hip, finding my blades. I closed my eyes, doing a mental inventory of the weapons I had on me. Hip. Ankle. Bra. Bracelet. Any place I could fit something sharp, I took full advantage. I needed to. Going in with the odds of three to one was already a risk. But hell, hadn't I faced so much more trying odds than that?

When I approached the side of the building, my confi-dence grew. How utterly careless were they to leave the door to the warehouse opened? Did they not expect that retribution would come for them? It has come, and it's a fury of anger and madness. I closed my eyes, letting the breeze ruffle my hair, letting stray strands lift and float for a moment, before I removed a hair tie from my wrist and pulled the strands back, balling them into a tight knot at the base of my neck.

I was ready.

Tightening the shadows like a cloak, I wrapped myself tightly, securing my invisibility as I stepped through the warehouse door. The scent inside was unexpected. Instead of death and decay and despair that coated this place like a thick layer of oil, the strands that assaulted my nose were pleasant. I took another whiff, inhaling deeply as I tried to separate each smell I was picking up. Cinnamon. Coffee. Cardamon. Smoke. Sage. Lavender. The scents were a surprise for sure. Their origin, still unknown.

The warehouse was dark, but in the far corner, a single light glowed. That was where I was headed, like a moth pulled toward a flame. I crept around the edges of the building, keeping my back to the wall. If my back was to the wall, I felt safer, not like anyone could see me. It was a tactic learned after years of being alone on the streets. Growing up as a mutant with no family wasn't easy, and I made my own way, despite the hardships.

I circled the building before nearing the light. It was empty, at least on the outside perimeter of the inside. But despite the quiet, I got the occasional clicking sound. I moved toward the sound, seeking answers. Wondering what in this darkness could make that noise. I moved slowly, each step weighed down by my desire for accuracy and stealth. My foot touched the cemented ground. Another click sounded. I waited, pausing for more, but came up with silence. I lifted my foot, not yet touching it to the ground to forward my steps when another click echoed.

I froze.

Did the clicks line up with my movements?

I let my foot touch the ground. Another click. My heart pace sped up. I had to be imagining it though, right? No one could see me; my body was covered in the black murky movement of the shadows. It was impossible. It was -

"Apples."

The voice boomed confidently through the warehouse, and I jumped, forgetting they couldn't see me for a moment. I let my body freeze in place, waiting for more but hoping for nothing. When the silence became heavy, I raised my foot again. The click sounded in rhythm with my step.

"Might as well come forward. We know you're here." The deep voice broke into the silence again. Was he talking to me? Impossible. Yet, with another click, he spoke again. "The shadows cannot hide you from me."

The tall man stepped into the light, a thin cane in his hand as his black eyes stared directly at me. But he saw nothing. He held no emotion or recognition in their depth, only pools of dark nothingness. Blind. He was blind. Yet, he found me when no one else had seen me before. He clicked his tongue again before he stepped in my direction.

Echolocation. I'd never seen it done before, but as he took a step closer, his head tilted. I knew his blank eyes saw more of me than anyone I'd ever met.

Did I speak? I shouldn't. If he hadn't really noticed me, speaking would ruin my safety. I needed out of here. I could come back. Maybe on a day where my shields hadn't been thrown for a loop and I wasn't feeling antsy and nervous. I took a step back with another click.

"You're not leaving." He closed his eyes and inhaled. "You smell like the freshest of apples. I bet you taste just as sweet."

If only he knew I was composed of sour and bitterness, he wouldn't look so infatuated. I swallowed hard. "I think I'm in the wrong place."

If all else fails, lie, and run, right? I'd never used that tactic, but I'd never ran into a problem like this before. Lie and run. It was literally the only thing I had now. Except I had weapons. Lots of weapons. I reached for my hip, and he cleared his throat, stopping me.

"I wouldn't do that."

Shit. How can he see so much? "I'll see myself out, thanks."

Fuck. See. Did I just unknowingly make a joke about seeing to a blind man? The slip up would have been hilarious under other circumstances, but now? With my heart racing and my palms sweating, the slip up was anything but funny. It was risky. Too fucking risky.

"That won't be necessary. You're here to kill us, right? But you must know you've got it all wrong."

Okay then. So, escaping this warehouse would surely not be done without a struggle. There was no way he would lie down and let me slash his throat willingly and we both know that's what I was here to do. Fuck it. I reached for my hip, grabbing hold of my knife. But I'd never had time to pull it free. A powerful arm wrapped around my throat, a shadow upon a shadow, and held me so tight I could barely swallow.

His nose rubbed into my hair before he lifted his face enough to mutter to the blind man, "Delicious apples."

Then, his grip tightened, cutting off my oxygen, and even though I struggled, fought against his strength as I reached for my weapon, my battle was lost, as I went limp in his arms.

CHAPTER
Three

WARREN

I knew someone would come. It was only a matter of time before the government tried again. And they would repeatedly try until we were dead. But together, it appears we are an unstoppable force. Thank fuck for that because I couldn't imagine a life without Rex and Ansel. I didn't want to imagine it.

I knew someone would come. I just never expected her.

I inhaled deeply before closing my eyes and savoring the scent of her, tasting every molecule of her makeup. She thought she was stealthy as she lurked away in the shadows, but we knew the moment she stepped into our building, stepped a single foot on our land, that she was here to kill us. We also knew she wouldn't succeed.

I stood over her, her body chained to a chair as I waited for her to wake. Her dagger twirled in my hand as I spun it about. She was loaded, weapons fitting in every space of her body that her clothing would allow. I had to admit, I admired her commitment to the kill. The thought was so fucking hot it sent a shiver down my spine.

Her eyes fluttered a few times before they opened and, in the light, I could see that they were a piercing electric blue, a stunning contrast against her black hair. I reached forward, my fingers toying with her long silky locks of black hair. Delicious. Absolute divinity. Mine. I already knew without a doubt I would own this mutant. Mine.

Her head jerked away from my touch. The chains rattled as she shifted. "Don't touch me."

"Possession is still nine-tenths of the law and right now I think it's proven that I own you." I smirked, seeing the disgust cross her face. She wouldn't feel that way for long.

"No one owns me." She tried to scoot further away from me, shaking her body until the chair we strapped her to scooted across the floor, moving her successfully into Rex.

His body shimmered as he allowed his facade to drop, no longer blending in with the background. She screamed, trying to move away as he leaned down close to her ears. "What's your name?"

He ran his split tongue down her ear, and she stretched as far as she could to pull away, still not answering. I didn't need an answer. I'd figure it out on my own. "Little Doe, are you going to tell us why you were sent here?"

I knew the reason. But did she know the truth? I doubted it. She shook her head. "Fuck off."

I'd rather fuck her, but in due time. "No name, no reason. What are we to do with you then?"

I leaned back against a table next to Ansel before crossing my arms. Her eyes burned into me. "I suspect you don't need me, so if you wanted to drop me off at the nearest gas station, I'd find my way home."

I laughed. "Little Doe, that's dangerous. You could get hurt."

She gave me a deadpan stare. "More hurt than hanging with the likes of you? I'd take my chances."

"And to drop you off, I bet you expect these back, wouldn't you?" I flipped a blade in my hand, skillfully catching it by the handle. "I wouldn't trust you not to stab me in the heart and though I do like a little blood play in the bedroom, I suspect you'd go for the kill."

"It's my job." She stated.

"Why?"

She laughed, her black locks falling forward and covering her from view. That wouldn't do. I closed the distance and knelt in front of her, before taking the hair in my hands and pulling it away so I could look into her eyes. "Why? Why is it my job to kill you?"

"Why are you killing mutants for them is the real question?" Ansel filled in.

"I'd kill anyone who harms others. Mutant or human." I saw into the depth of her eyes, and I knew she believed it.

I dropped her hair and stood, turning my back to her. "They lie to you. You know that don't you?"

She laughed, then had the nerve to spit at me. I felt my cock stir at the audacity. "And I'm supposed to what? Believe you? The person I'm sent after. Is this what you told the other agents before you murdered them?"

"That's offensive." I spat while using the tip of her dagger to pierce my finger. At least she used sharp weapons. Good girl. "You assumed we let the others come this far and get this close to us, and that just isn't the case. No little Doe. We slaughtered them instantly."

She pulled against the rope, and I knew she was trying to get her hands free. I also knew she would succeed. I'd seen determination in her eyes. This girl wouldn't give up until the very last breath had left her body. She didn't know that I'd never let it get that far. Sometimes precious things are worth the protection, even if they don't realize they have value.

"Why am I here?" She glared. "Why am I not slaughtered instantly?"

Cute. The mockery of her voice was fucking adorable. Rex rubbed a hand down her neck affectionately, "I can't speak for them, but I know for a fact you're here because I want my cock down your throat."

"Disgusting." she hissed and used her head to bat his hand away.

I sat her dagger down next to Ansel and rubbed my hands together. "What do you know about our kind?"

"I am nothing of your kind." She sneered.

"You're being dense, Doe."

"Don't call me that." I loved when she growled.

"You know, us mutants are all the same at our core. Are you going to deny that?" I pursed my lips as I waited for a response.

It took a while for her to answer and for a moment, I thought she wouldn't. But finally, she sighed, slightly defeated, and admitted the truth. "I know a little."

"Enough to know you're a rare omega." Her eyes widened when I spoke the information and she suddenly fought harder against the restraints, as if that would help her be free. It wouldn't. And even if she had managed, there was no way to get past us. I continued speaking, "The government doesn't want us to continue our line. They don't want us to breed or build a larger population than those they created. They don't see that it's already happening."

"I'm not-"

"You are." My voice boomed, borderline loud enough that to some, it might be considered yelling. "You are an omega and though you deny it, your scent and our very real reaction to it prove that fact. It's funny really, sort of clever, that they would use the very being we sought to attempt at our demise."

"Is that why you traffic all those women and children?" Her growl was nearly as powerful as my own.

"What? No. Is that what they told you?" That was appalling.

"Where are you keeping them?" She demanded.

"The people I've saved?" I couldn't help but laugh. "I've tucked them away, protecting them from the unfair persecution."

"I wish I believed your lie."

I couldn't help but step toward her. She drew me to the nearness. It was her scent. It begged me to touch her. My fingers picked up another lock of hair and I rubbed it in my hand. I wondered how long it took her to grow her hair this long. Sheets of it laid down her back stopping at her waist. It would be exquisite to pull while my cock was buried inside of her.

I tore myself from my thoughts. "Believe them. The only thing stopping you from believing my truths are the lies that the government had planted. I suspect deep down you know they are true. Don't you? I have no reason to lie to you, little Doe. It serves me no purpose."

"Show me proof." She demanded.

I dropped the hair in favor of grabbing her chin, forcing her eyes to look at me. "What proof do you need?"

"Where do you put the women and children?"

"I've told you, safely tucked away."

"Show me." She demanded while she stared into my very soul with those eyes of electricity.

I forced myself to drop her chin. "I can't. I want to, but you have to understand, you're working for the enemy."

"I work for myself. The enemy, as you say, just contracts me."

"I could contract you." Rex added to the conversation.

"She isn't a sex worker, Rex." Ansel defended the girl before pausing. "Wait, you aren't, right?"

She scrunched up her nose in disgust. "No."

Rex lowered his body to the floor as he muttered a curse under his breath. With no respect for her personal space, he scooted closer to her, aligning his body with her denim clad leg. He didn't care that she looked down on him in disgust, but also didn't realize that by doing what he was doing at this very moment, he was marking. Rubbing his scent against her body and claiming her as ours. There were many ways we planned on marking this omega, many ways indeed. But this, right here, was the first of many. There was no disputing that fact.

I let my hand fall to Rex's head for a moment, letting his hair slide through my fingers as I pulled away. "I can show you, but it has to be tomorrow. I've got a meeting today."

"If I don't get back to check in, they'll send someone else after you." She seemed proud. "I hope you know that. The next person wouldn't fail."

"She's dramatic." Ansel observed. "But her heart rate says she worries about the outcome of this situation."

"We've no plans to kill you, Doe."

"Don't call me that." She snapped.

"Your name, then?" She refused to speak, only glared at me with her teeth clinched. "No matter, I'll find out for myself, eventually. If it's your absence you worry about, I'll let you go."

"You will?" Rex's purr against her leg drowned out her question.

"Sure." I walked over to her and sliced the rope that bound her arm, knowing she had no weapons to fight me. She didn't move, though. She was suspicious. "Come back here tomorrow, little Doe. I'll take you to the people."

"If I don't?" She swallowed hard.

"If you don't, we will find you. There is not a corner of this earth that we wouldn't be able to locate you now." I stated.

"This goes without saying, I assume, but even so, come alone."

I knew she would come alone because deep down, she had questions, and we had answers. She wanted to trust the government and hope that their actions were truthful, but she didn't. And with good reason too, because wasn't it the government and their deceit who created the monsters like us?

"How do I know you won't hurt me?" She questioned, and I wondered if she realized she used her free hand to rub against Rex's scalp as she watched me with suspicion. Yes. She was perfect for us, already scent marking what was hers.

"We could have hurt you now, but we didn't." I pointed out.

"You choked me out." She looked down and realized what she was doing. She pulled her hand away like she had touched fire. "That was harm."

"Hardly. That was a precaution. There isn't a mark on your body to prove otherwise. Though I would willingly volunteer to do a thorough check if there are concerns."

"Disgusting creep."

I beamed. "Tomorrow then. Nine o'clock."

She bent down to pull at the ropes at her ankles. "Fine. Nine. I want my weapons back."

I laughed. Smart girl. Though we both knew she wasn't getting them back. "Not a chance."

"I have more anyway." She grumbled under her breath as she pulled the final rope free and, well, I wouldn't expect anything less. "This better not be a trap."

"I've no reason to trap you." I turned my back on her, walking away, knowing she wouldn't attack. The seed of doubt had been planted. Our scent now marked her skin. She wouldn't harm us. "Until tomorrow, Doe. Sleep tight."

CHAPTER
Four

ANSEL

I couldn't see her walk away, but I felt her. I felt her part away from us and I wanted to chase her, force her back, put those ropes and chains on her and not let her go. But Warren decided, and who was I to question the leader in our group. Especially when, even if I disagreed, I knew his decision was the best one.

"You let her go." Rex voiced what I didn't want to.

"I had to." Warren admitted. "It was hard as fuck to do, too."

"Then why did you?" I asked.

"If we let her go, and she comes back, it means she truly, deep down, trusts what we say to be true." Warren stood at the door, staring into the night. She was long gone, not even bothering to wrap herself in the shadows as she walked down the pavement. Not like the shadows hid her from us. The scent of the omega was strong with her. The scent was damn near heaven.

"But if she doesn't come back?" Rex seemed nearly

distraught about the prospect of that. He was the tender one of the group.

"If she doesn't come back, I'll do what I promised. I'll hunt her down."

My body shivered with the excitement of it. I loved a good hunt, and when it came to hunting her, I hoped he would let me participate. I still had to wonder what the plans were if she came back. "Are you going to show her?"

"Yes." I could hear Warren move. I clicked my tongue, listening to his location so I could face him.

"It's risky."

"They want us dead, Ansel. They want us dead, and they are portraying us as the bad guys." He simply stated.

Sometimes, we were the bad guys. But only if the situation called for it. This situation? We were definitely good. "You think taking her to our most protected secret will change her mind?"

"Why wouldn't it? She will see firsthand that we aren't trafficking, we are protecting. Building. Communizing those who are different. The government wants us dead because we are protecting our people when they failed to do so. They would rather us drop off this earth and all die than admit they were wrong in creating and mutating us. We are doing the work they refused to do." I heard Warren's pants ruffle, and I knew he had stuck his hands in his pocket. "Besides, I think she liked us."

I had to laugh at that. "If you handed that dagger back to her, she would have tried to slit your throat."

He groaned his approval. "I would have loved every second. I can't wait to see what she brings to play with tomorrow. She didn't realize she was doing it, but she was letting Rex mark her. She even toyed with his hair some."

I smiled. "Our omega is already growing soft toward us."

"I wouldn't call it soft." Warren commented. "But she will."

"She went this long without knowing her rarity. Do you think the government knew?" I asked.

"They had to have known." Rex commented. "Keeping her close and keeping her in their employment means they can have a close eye on her, track her whereabouts."

"Why not just kill her?" The thought of it, as I spoke it out loud, made my stomach sour. She was mine. Ours. Her death would be unacceptable. It would be avenged even if we hardly knew her.

"Curiosity." Warren commented. "Maybe they wanted to see how long before she discovered what she was."

"She's in danger." I pointed out. "And she doesn't even know it."

"She doesn't and for now, she could be safe. They don't know we recognize her for what she is. Once they find out, that's when her trouble begins. I'll not let them get to her." His voice shifted toward Rex. "Watch her apartment. Just in case." Rex didn't have to be told twice. He already shifted to move out of the room. But before he left, Warren spoke again. "Invisible please. We don't want to be drawing attention to our fascinations."

"I'll blend in." He informed Warren, then his steps faded away.

"What's your plan if she does show up? Just take her underground? That could risk leading people back to us."

"I'll blindfold her."

A laugh rumbled from my chest. "You do like blindfolds."

"Aye, I do." He laughed. "But I won't let her see where we are going. I just hope her sense of direction is shit."

I doubted her sense of direction was anything but impeccable, but we would have to take precautions and attempt to confuse her. She moved through the shadows and through the night as if she was one with everything dark around her. Silent and lethal. Perfection. Delicious perfection. If it wasn't for her scent that hit us so damn strong, I never would have known she had entered the warehouse.

"We should take a few extra routes, just to be sure." I suggested.

"I was thinking the same." Warren reached toward the door of the warehouse, the movement sending tiny ripples through the air toward me. I heard his hand clamp down on the handle before the metal of the door dragged against the cement. The door slammed heavily before Warren turned his attention back to me. "We've got a full twenty-four hours ahead of us. Feel up to some drinks?"

The sunset of the following day filled Warren with anticipation. According to Rex, who stared into her window the whole time, going completely unseen, the girl did nothing but sit at her desk, staring at the folders in front of her. Folders of us. Folders filled with lies of discretions we had never partaken in and information that was never verified.

She paced.

She drank, though she barely ate, which Rex thought would need to be fixed as soon as possible.

She contemplated.

And as the sun went down and the surrounding air became cooler, the man closest to me became more agitated. Though the facade he wore was confident, I knew he worried she wouldn't come. He didn't want to track her down. Tracking her down meant unleashing a beast inside of him, one that didn't want to chase her for the fun and thrill of the game, but who wanted to claim her. Mark her inside like we had already done on the outside. He wanted her dripping with his scent, and it was too soon for that. She would resist for sure.

The phone on the desk buzzed, and I answered it before hitting the speaker. "Yeah?"

"She's on her way." Rex spoke and relief filled me. "How she can fit so many weapons on such a tiny body is beyond my comprehension but be aware of them."

Warren snorted. He liked the games he already knew she would play. He liked to be the cat chasing the mouse. And I knew he secretly hoped she would use one of those daggers or the tiny hidden blades against his skin. "When will she be here?"

"She's about ten minutes out."

The line went dead, and I knew Rex was following her. I wonder if she could sense him as much as we could sense her presence. Did she spend the entire day ignoring him at her window, or did she truly believe we would send her back home unprotected? The minutes ticked by, and Warren became more restless. He tried to pretend like his eyes weren't glued to the door, but even blind, he couldn't fool me. I knew, I knew everything about him and because of that, I've memorized his mannerisms.

"I see her."

"She isn't in the shadows?" Interesting.

"No. She is just walking like normal." He seemed shocked by that, too.

"Probably figured you knew she was coming. The shadows are useless." I pointed out.

"But she wouldn't want the agency to know she's coming. Right?" He asked.

"Unless she wanted cameras and proof of where she was headed."

He growled. "She's too fucking smart. It's infuriatingly hot."

"We won't be here long enough for it to matter. We'll be on the move soon."

The sound of gravel under her boots seeped into the silence of the night, drawing out the lull of the ocean nearby. It grew louder, each step taken with purpose, each step held anger as she slammed her foot down. Her scent wafted in through the doorway and I knew I couldn't be the only one to feel my cock instantly stir at the appeal. Apples. Apples and spices and fresh baked pie, and it was a delicious combination I hadn't consumed in years.

"Your dog has been watching me all day." She accused and I guess that answered the question of if she knew Rex was nearby.

"And night." Warren goaded.

"I'd appreciate some privacy." She sighed. "And also, you all are fucking creepy."

Creeps? No. Obsessive? Maybe a little. But it wasn't our fault. The change from human to mutant did it to us, made us crave a specific type of being. It wasn't our fault that her DNA had changed her into that being what we all wanted so damn badly.

"I appreciate you coming tonight." Warren stated, and I knew he had to fight the urge not to touch her. Hell, even I had to fight the urge and I was the less sociable of the three.

"I didn't come for you." She stated.

"I never dreamed that you would have." Warren replied instantly, and it was true. He was under no illusion that wherever this was going would be an easy ride. She learned a lot of lies about us, was conditioned to believe the lies they told. But now it was our turn to show her the truth. To show her all the things she had once believed about our kind, was propaganda to hide the truth.

Superiority.

We were the superior beings now and if they were going to suppress that fact, then we had to make it known.

"I'm curious." she admitted.

We knew she would be. Her eyes screamed with curiosity and her actions, the way she poured over the files for hours on end, only spoke of her need for answers. But the answers, she would never find them in a file they handed to her. The answers would never be accessible to her because they viewed her as a tool. But to us, she was an asset.

"The government would tell you curiosity killed the cat, and for them, that is true. But for us, it leads to enlightenment. Knowledge you hadn't been gifted before." Warren's foot shuffled against the pavement. "We need to blindfold you."

"Absolutely not." I heard her take a step back and her body hit into Rex. He purred his contentment.

"We can't have you giving away our location."

"You think a blindfold will stop me?" She huffed her disagreement.

"You can keep the knives." Warren paused. "You won't stab us."

"You're so confident that I won't." I heard her heart pick up pace, and I knew she was nervous.

"I hope you will." He muttered, and I knew that if I could see there would be a standoff happening right in front of me. A visual of them eye fucking each other as they stood toe to toe in their own stubborn states.

Finally, she sighed, "Fine. I'll wear a blindfold. But I won't hesitate to kill you if you bring me into anything shady."

"I never doubted that you would hesitate for a single second, little Doe."

Then I heard the rustle of fabric as Warren removed the blindfold from his pocket and felt the tension as he tied it around her eyes. She was blind. We were the same. Our senses heightened by the deduction of one. Could she hear better? Smell stronger? Did every single fabric that now touched against her fingertips have ridges and weaves she could distinguish?

"I'm going to touch your arm now." Warren informed her.

"I'd rather you didn't." She seethed the words, and I loved the bite she put behind them.

"Well, I'd rather your pretty little skin not be covered in

bruises by the end of the night." I clicked my tongue and listened, knowing that Warren was now standing directly next to her, his body only an inch away. "I'd rather the bruises be left by my hands only."

Another click and I could tell she stepped away. "Gross."

"It's a matter of time, Doe. Just a matter of time." He was confident in his confession, rightfully so. She would soften to us. She was made for us, after all.

"Lead the way, Warren." She demanded. "But touch nothing but my elbow."

He groaned his satisfaction. "I do love the sound of my name rolling off your tongue."

CHAPTER
Five

THEA

I would not admit out loud that I enjoyed the feel of Warren's hands against my skin. They were warm and large. Everything about these men was large. They dwarfed me, hovering over me with their looming height while all I could do was stand straight and pretend that I wasn't the slightest bit intimidated. But I was. The personalities that surrounded me were strong, and I hadn't yet known what it was about them that made them so damn powerful that the government wanted them dead.

"Did you kill the agents?" I asked.

I couldn't see their faces, not when I was blindfolded as they led me through the abandoned subway tunnels, like I wouldn't be able to figure that out.

"They struck first." Warren simply stated.

"If they hadn't?" I prompted.

"They still would have died." Ansel said.

I turned toward his voice as he clicked his tongue. The

sound was soothing as he found his way through the tunnels independently. "You didn't kill me."

"You are ours." Rex said simply, as if that was the truth and there was no argument. I had plenty of arguments.

"I'm not." The words left my mouth as a harsh rumble.

"You are." Warren's fingers tightened on my elbow as he pulled me around a curve. I don't know why he bothered blindfolding me. I could pinpoint where we were. I could tell him the exact location. Even if he spent half our travels trying to throw me off by taking unnecessary turns and routes. "They were human. You are an omega mutant."

"I don't truly know what that means, and I think by now you three know that and are taunting me with that fact." I pointed out as Warren pulled me to the side to avoid what had to be some fallen bricks.

"It means you're ours." Rex spoke again. Bless him for his obsessive personality. Unfortunately, he didn't speak the truth about this one.

"Rex is correct."

"Rex is certainly not correct." My voice, louder than it should be, echoed through the tunnel.

"He is, indeed." Warren spoke. "There are very few females that can breed and reproduce with us. We were made, Doe. They altered our DNA with their experimental shots, ensuring they were safe. Now, some children are born by default with mutant defects. But mutants can't have children under normal circumstances, unless... they have an omega."

Though I knew some of what he spouted were facts, the breeding of an omega seemed preposterous. It was known that mutants cannot reproduce, and why would they want to? We were flawed. Broken. So many defects that it was hard to keep track of what was normal these days. The thought of reproducing and creating monsters like us never crossed my mind. "That's a lie."

"It absolutely isn't a lie." Warren sounded angry at my

rejection. "There are few people, few mutants, that could do what I asked, and you're one of them, Doe."

"I think you have the wrong girl. You're so fucking delusional, Warren, that you would believe any rumor that came your way. Even if it was true, which it isn't, I wouldn't be the omega."

I was just an orphaned girl trying to get by in a lonely as fuck world. I wasn't made to have friends, and I wasn't a mothering, nurturing type. I wouldn't even know where to address how much of an absolute clusterfuck their ideas of me and my future were. "Even if this is true, and I want to stress with you three how much it isn't, I don't want to be a mother. I never want children."

"We do." Rex sighed.

Shit, he was like a hopeful puppy.

"It's not just about children, though I won't deny, I would love burying my cock inside of you." I scrunched up my face, disgusted. "It's about the hope you bring. Did we expect the next person to try to take our heads to be you? Absolutely not. But the moment we got your scent, we knew what you were and that, well, sealed our obsession and our decisions on how to proceed."

"I wish I could tell you you're not filled with delusions, but I think we both know you're more delusional than the man spouting prophecies by the corner store on ninth street." I stated, nearly tripping on the slippery gravel under my feet. Warren's grip tightened, not allowing me to fall.

"Maybe so, but I suspect you see that I speak the truth." He inhaled deep, then slowly exhaled. "Because of the unique ability you have, we can prove to the humans that we are worthy of the life they are trying to snuff out."

"They aren't snuffing you out." I defended the very people who paid my bills. "We only go after the bad guys, the ones who break the law."

"Like the businessman killed last week. That was you,

wasn't it? I got a hint of apple at the scene and thought nothing of it at the time. He wasn't breaking any laws, Doe. He was ready to break a story about the superiority of mutant DNA."

"No." I stated firmly. That wasn't true. "He was responsible for the murders of four attorneys and five civilians. He was a serial killer."

"He never killed a fly in the years I knew him." Ansel stated.

"You don't know everything about a person just because you think you know who they are." I felt Warren tug on my arm, and we turned around a curve.

"Steps." He informed me and I lifted my foot in time to not trip. "And you don't know a person in all their capacity based on a government file handed to you in a manilla folder with a name marked in sharpie."

"It's printed." I added, feeling a little salty because, as much as I didn't want to admit it, he was right. I didn't know everything about the man I killed. I knew where he would be, a little about his habits, and the crime for which he was gifted his execution.

"It makes no difference." He guided me up the steps. "He was an innocent man you deemed guilty based off a folder given to you by the government. The same government that told you we traffic mutants."

"Do you?" I asked, even though I knew they already denied it.

"We would never dream of it." Rex spoke first and damn it, coming from him, it seemed like an impossibility now. He seemed the gentlest of the three, less judging and...

"Rex, didn't you choke me out?" I remember just as I was sort of feeling fond of the giant.

"I was protecting you." He said it like he believed it.

"From?"

"If you had pulled a knife on us, I'd have had to kill you. I didn't want that. I hate killing."

I grunted as I hit the top step. "You're so fucking kind."

"Thank you." Rex accepted the backhanded compliment proudly.

I was feeling a bit sensitive at this point. My mind was reeling with the possibility that maybe they were correct. I didn't want to entertain the thought, but if I had murdered a man, a mark, because the government created lies about a man, I would feel awful. Hell, the possibility of it already had my stomach turning. But no. I would not let these men get into my head. They were creating issues where there was none. I had every reason to trust the government and not to trust the mutants that surrounded me. Except-

Sometimes I did question the government. Sometimes I wondered what the hell they thought to accomplish by killing off some marks. I questioned some things I heard muttered in the last seconds before a soul left a body. I questioned the truth in the last moments. I questioned my reality versus theirs.

"Where are you taking me?" I demanded.

It was a dumb demand. We had been walking for over an hour and just now I was wondering where I was going? No. I knew where we were heading, but I wanted the subject changed. I didn't want to entertain the thought that I might carry on the race of people I could hardly relate to. I wasn't raised in a situation where I had access to mutants and learned about the things they could do firsthand. I raised myself in the streets, begging for food and doing anything I could to feed myself.

I picked life.

My life.

My life over anyone.

And I'd continue to do so.

"We're taking you home." Ansel's voice broke into the silence.

"The 76th street station is your home?" I muttered, and I felt their bodies freeze.

"I don't understand what you're talking about." Warren tried.

"I bet you don't." I looked his way, even though I couldn't see him through the blindfold. "If you wanted to throw me off, you probably should have tried a little harder."

"We took detoured routes. You were blindfolded." Ansel muttered.

"You hardly tried." They tried hard for sure, but I would not give them credit. "You made a few extra turns."

"We made twenty detours!" Ansel's voice rose. "How were we supposed to know you had the whole subway mapped in your head?"

"Actually, 76th street station isn't technically on the map." I pointed out.

"We're aware." They all said in unison.

"But to be fair, the entire city is up here." I tapped my temple. "You never would have tricked me unless we left the area."

Warren's hand traveled from my elbow down to my hand, where he grabbed it. "What are you doing?"

He pushed my palm onto his hard dick. "This is what you do to me. Your fucking genius and smart-ass mouth make me hard as a fucking rock."

It took a good three seconds for his words to register and the feeling of his large member under my fingers to sink in. I pulled my hand back, pulling away from him. "You're disgusting."

"I'm in love." He mumbled.

"You're crazy. And obsessive. You need a psychologist." I declared.

His hand found my hip, and he pulled me toward him.

His mouth was so close to my ear as he muttered, "I'm only obsessed with you. That I can promise."

He bit down on my earlobe and fuck, I would not admit it out loud, especially to him, but a full body shiver overtook me. I used my palm to push at his chest and he pushed back easy enough, not trying to hide his laugh of amusement. The fucking bastard knew I liked what he did, and I hated my body for betraying me.

Rex cleared his throat. "I guess we don't need the blind-fold, then."

A hand reached up, and the blindfold fell away and we were walking in the dark depth of the shadows. The shadows, my home. A place where I could feel completely comfortable and at home. My eyes needed no time to adjust. The dark was a part of them.

"They glow." Rex said in fascination as he looked at me and suddenly, I was hit with a wave of self-consciousness.

"Hum." Warren observed. "Interesting."

"What?" I demanded.

"When you don't have the shadows wrapped around you, your eyes glow like a nightlight." Rex informed me before he rubbed a hand to his chin.

"It makes me want to mate her harder." Warren added.

"I am fucking done with you, Warren." I pointed a finger to the other side of Rex and Ansel. "There. Stand there."

The strength of lust Warren had laid on me was annoying, but also, I enjoyed the attention. Though I'd never utter that out loud. It was a lonely life lurking in the shadows, assassinating criminals at the government's whim. And though I had friends, the few I had were coworkers. I clearly had issues having a life outside of work.

Warren moved to the other side of Rex, and I looked, my surroundings dark and damp in the underground tunnels. Graffiti covered the walls, stray papers laid upon the ground and aluminum cans were scattered. Aluminum, those were worth a nice penny these days. What once was so disposable had become a government asset. "You should sell those cans back to the government. They are going for nearly five bucks each."

Warren gave me a look that told me he clearly wasn't amused, but it was Ansel who spoke. "We could, but we don't need the money. We'll leave it to someone who is homeless and needs the funds."

I pursed my lips. "So generous of you."

"I'm generous in other ways." Warren added.

I couldn't hide my sneer. "Pass."

He only laughed. The man was fully aware he was going overboard with his come-ons and I doubted he planned to stop. I walked ahead of them slightly, somehow not fearing that I willingly had my enemies at my back. If what they say about me is true, which I doubt, they wouldn't want to kill me unless they truly had to. I'm not convinced of the validity of their information, and they could just be leading me around under the city, in dark dank tunnels for their own amusement, before they slaughter me. Though, they didn't bother taking any of my knives this time.

A rat passed my feet, scurrying with a piece of treasure grasped in its jaw. They were massive down here, sized as big as a cat and I tried not to focus on them, or scream when they were near. I could kill a man, his blood dripping through my fingers, but the sight of a rat too close making me squirm? I would lose all forms of credibility.

We reached a long platform, one built for waiting passengers to board a train that never once saw the feet of scurrying passengers. "There was a ladder, but they are no longer serviceable. We will have to hike you up to the platform."

It was Warren's voice that had broken the silent bubble around us. "You just want to touch my butt."

"Though true, it's also not the case in these circumstances." The boys all stopped in unison. "Ansel will go up first."

As much as I didn't want a single bone in my body to soften toward these men, I couldn't help it. They instinctively let Ansel go first, knowing he couldn't see. It was protective. If this tunnel was used and a service cart came by, it would have been easier for everyone to escape the danger because they would have seen it coming, except Ansel. But I knew he would have heard a cart before anyone saw it.

He didn't need help to lift himself up. I doubt any of the men did. Every movement they made, their muscles bunched and rolled and getting up on the platform was no different. They had done it before. Countless times if their swiftness had anything to do with it. He used his height to his advantage and sprung upward. And, well shit, I told myself I would not look, but my eyes wouldn't tear away from him.

When he was standing, Warren looked toward me. "Your turn, Doe."

I opened my mouth to object, but he gave me no time for the words to leave my mouth. His hands were on my waist, and he already had me in the air. It was impressive, his strength, and damn it, I let him manhandle me up onto the platform because even with all the denial I was willing to spout, I was shorter than they were. I didn't have the advantage of height to help me when hoisting myself up. My feet met the tile and Ansel's hands grabbed hold.

Seconds later, Rex and Warren were beside me. Their movement was so swift I hadn't even seen them rise from below the platform. Without a word, Rex led the way, and I followed. Ansel trailed behind me, with Warren closing out the back. Rex led us further into the station, and I felt like I was in a twisted time warp. Rarely are the subways used any longer. They shut down years ago when mutants surfaced, and the world changed. The change was not for the better.

But this station looked lost in time, long before the rest had shut down. Its walls were grey, the paint, whatever the original color once was, had long chipped away, leaving only exposed cement. The graffiti was faded and reapplied. Layers upon layers of art, of expression, of someone's soul dripping out onto the walls because their soul couldn't drip out to a single person.

I knew the feeling. The loneliness. The despair of knowing you had no one to talk to.

And when we follow the cracks in the busted pavement like one would a map, or a constellation of scars, there are secret hearts speaking minor symphonies.

I ran my fingers over the painted words, wondering about the soul who painted them. How long ago did their words bleed onto this surface of wood boarding, then were left here to rot like their surroundings? Did their souls still bleed, or had they healed from the wounds that plagued them?

"It's a little further this way." Warren spoke, breaking the silence. The words echoed into the nothingness and my spine tingled with the sudden chill it brought.

We turned a corner, the sight just as heartbreaking as the stretch we left behind. "Why underground?"

I hadn't meant to ask, but the words slipped out of my mouth anyway. Warren, more serious than I'd seen him, was the one who spoke. "When you're a mutant, a monster, the very thing people fear in their dreams, it's better to be unseen. To stay hidden and safe."

I wondered what exactly made these men monsters. Sure, I could guess and say that the light green and purple scales that crept up Rex's neck and his ability to blend with his surroundings made him sort of a reptile species, chameleon like. And the blindness, echolocation with Ansel made me wonder if he might have some sort of chiropteran mutations. But Warren, I've gotten no signs that he was anything but normal. Well, not mentally. He's proven repeatedly to be one crayon short of a box. But why would he call himself a mutant? Was it rude to ask?

"Hidden and safe. Is that what you want for your people?"

"No." He answered honestly as he turned to look at me. "Your eyes make my heart nearly stop."

And here I was, trying to have a serious conversation. I ignored him. "Then what do you want?"

"It's not merely what I want. It's not that simple. It's what we deserve. We may hide, and we hide well, but we want to be seen. We were the people of this nation. The people who stepped up when the government promised us safety then got disregarded when their promises were proven false. We aren't trash, Doe. They hunt us, you hunt us, because they believe we are lower than the lowest class citizens of the human race. We deserve a chance, and we aren't getting it."

My stomach rolled at the thought that what he spoke might have been true. Had I hunted people like myself for no reason? It couldn't be true. I needed to ask the few acquaintances I had if they find this to be an accurate assessment. Maybe Warren was only playing a victim in a victimless crime. Had I known this might be the case, it would have been something I never participated in.

"What do you want?" I asked again because it was simple.

This time, he didn't hesitate when he answered. "Control."

It was what I feared. But handing over control to a person like Warren, a person who already radiated power, was out of the question. I'd seen what he could do. I'd seen photos of my fellow fallen marksmen, and it was horrifying. I wouldn't wish their deaths on anyone and that says so fucking much when you're a government trained assassin.

"I'd poke out my own eyes with a flaming iron poker before I handed you over control."

He laughed. Warren had the nerve to laugh when I was so painfully serious. "Oh, I want control, but not in the way you may think, my little Doe. Control of the people? No, that doesn't interest me. Control of your body as my cock is knotted and spurting inside of you? Well, that is the only control a man like me really needs."

Fuck.

Fuck.

Fuck.

Why did that statement have my core throbbing and my body instantly igniting with sparks of want?

"Fuck off." I nearly growled the words, trying not to sound breathless. "There is not a chance in hell that you would find your way into this body."

He sighed, but not in defeat. "There is a clear misunderstanding, my little Doe. I would not find my way into your body. Your body would beg me with flashing lights and a personal invitation."

Fuck.

I hoped we never got to a point where he would prove me wrong because, hell, I've known him less than a day and already his voice was like a siren call.

I turned to Rex. "He seems to have forgotten I am prolific with weapons."

Rex just laughed. "No, I think that fact only spurs him on more."

Well, fuck. I was screwed.

CHAPTER
Six

REX

I tried not to smell her hair as she walked near me. That would be creepy, right? Not like it mattered. When a mutant of her capabilities gets gifted to you, you can't really be held accountable for the actions you do toward her. It was hard not to touch her. I wanted to touch her every second. It was hard to watch where I was going when my eyes only drifted in her direction.

I wasn't like Warren, who was powerful and strong and made his dominance known. In a hierarchy, he was a true alpha. And Ansel, despite his inability to see, was the protector. He looked innocent enough, but he was as vicious as they come, and people underestimated what he could do. He was the strongest delta I'd ever seen, truly a hidden powerhouse of strength and power. But me, I was a lover, not a fighter. The beta in my blood ran through me so thick that to lift a hand in true violence made me want to be physically ill.

But I'd do it.

I'd do anything for her.

She didn't even realize we were gaining her trust. Through her sneers and objections, she grew comfortable. She no longer held a hand near her knife, or always kept her eyes on us, and she may not have realized this, but her arm kept brushing against mine as we walked and when I leaned into her, she didn't lean away.

"This way." Warren growled, as she almost stepped into a tiny pothole. His hand snaked out, pulled her toward him so fast she had no time to fight.

He was obsessed. Infatuated. One scent of her as she laid limp in my arm, and he nearly went wild with lust. To hold back? Well, that had been his greatest challenge. He made no secret of his intentions, though. He wanted her. He craved her. He absolutely would have her now. It wasn't a matter of if, because to Warren, she belonged to us. It was a matter of when she came around and aligned her wants with ours.

"I could do without your touch." She seethed.

"You would have fallen." His dismay echoed through the hollow space.

"It would have been worth the injury." She glared at him and though the fun had just begun, I knew at some point the two would ignite into the hottest of flames.

"I will not have you getting hurt." His brows creased.

"You almost killed me." That was false. The moment we scented her in the air, killing her was never a factor. Even now, when Warren says he would do what he must do if the situation calls for it, I knew he wouldn't be able to. He was attached and when Warren got attached, he attached himself strongly.

"Females are so dramatic." Warren groaned. "We hardly hurt you."

"My wrists are bruised from the restraints, and they drew blood." She held her wrists up in the air, though the surrounding darkness made it nearly impossible to see any injuries.

Warren grabbed her wrists and kissed them both before she could pull away. "It was never our intention. Your struggle was a contribution."

Her electrifying eyes rolled up at his show of affection, clearly not impressed. "Victim blaming?"

I had to cut in, knowing that Warren went in too strong and too strong could tear her away from us before we even fully had her. "See that wall?"

"Yeah?" She stared at a brick structure straight ahead.

"It's false. That's our entrance."

She watched me suspiciously for a moment while the sound of Ansel's clicks filled the silence. Finally, she spoke. "Promise you won't kill me if I follow you in there?"

"Would a promise make you more confident in your safety?" I wanted to nuzzle in her neck and wrap her strands of black hair around my body like a cloak. I was aware of how creepy that was, but I couldn't help it. She was the dream we had long wished for, but thought would never come true. And she was here, standing next to me as we walked through the dark.

"From you three, probably not." She admitted.

"Then I won't make a promise and you'll have to trust that your safety is our top priority." I stated as we reached the brick wall.

We stopped in front of it, and she took a few steps away from us, rubbing her arms nervously. At least she wasn't holding a dagger. That had to be something in our favor. Warren counted the bricks and for a moment, I thought maybe, he would give some caution since she was here. But he pressed down, and the brick wall pulled away from the structure.

Ansel held out an arm to her, and reluctantly, she grasped it before entering. When they were just far enough that they couldn't hear me, I asked. "No safety precautions when opening? What if she leads them back?"

Warren didn't even turn in my direction as he spoke. His eyes were solely on the back of the girl in front of us. "I trust she won't betray us."

"I'd like to trust in the same but trusting someone we just met based on lust is never a good idea. Warren, you put them all at risk."

His voice was hard when he spoke again. "You question me?"

"I don't question your decisions, ever. I just wanted to make sure you were clear on the potential outcomes of those decisions." And it was true if he thought this was a good idea. I'd believe it, too. But believing in his ability to decide and worrying about the outcome of these decisions were two different things.

"If we don't give her trust, she won't be drawn back." He stated.

"What does that even mean?"

"When she leaves here tonight, I want her to come back. I want her to find us. I want her to be close to us. I can't have these things if she is wary of our intentions. We trusted her with what's most important to us, our people. She needs to trust us with what's most important to her."

I turned to look at him, his eyes burning as he watched her. The fire simmering just under his skin. "Which is what, Warren?"

"Herself." He whispered.

The hallway was dark and though she probably thought she was helping Ansel navigate the hall that led to the opening where our people lived, I knew it was the other way around. He was guiding her, keeping her close in case he needed to protect her, or worse, protect them from her. His tongue clicked as he moved, the sound echoing off the wall. He didn't even need to perform the task any longer. He knew each step down this walkway by heart. Each risen tile or misplaced stone was embedded in our memories.

And it should be.

It should be embedded into every fiber of our being because it was those flaws that started it all for us. It was walking down through this darkness as scared, lonely teens that began the building of something greater. There wasn't life under this city. No, the life underground died years before the subways stopped. But with the flow of mutants growing and the prejudice against them increasing, the world had no choice but to adapt and grow. The world, being the mutants who built their own way.

It was a city, and it was large. It strived and depended on working together and it didn't matter what you looked like, underground you were equal. Underground, you were worthy. Underground, your life held no less of a value than the person next to you.

Like he had done so many times in the years since our childhood, Ansel's hand reached out and grasped a bar. He pushed the bar down before pulling it out, opening the last shield our people had against the world. The doorway opened into a chamber, larger than one could imagine. It was cavernous, and it took countless people and years to even carve out a space this large in the underground.

Our little Doe gasped, "It's so large."

"That's what she said." Warren winked, and I knew he was fucking proud of himself. He showed her his biggest secret, the thing he kept near to his heart, and gave her an obnoxious pickup line without missing a single beat.

She glared at him, not acknowledging his comment. Then she turned away, taking in the space that seemed to be endless. She hadn't even realized that though we had brought her up on the platform earlier, that platform was just a first step into a slowly descending earth. A single millimeter at a time was so unnoticeable of a difference until you were down deep into the earth. Her head tilted back as she looked above us, the space faintly lit by borrowed electricity from the city above.

"This is…"

"Amazing? I know." Warren cut her off confidently. "If you follow a little further in, you'll see why it's so important."

We didn't have the greatness of the place visible when you entered. There was a freestanding wall blocking the view of people. But another few feet and she would see it. A town. A community. A union built not on will, but necessity. Dwellings, and dorms, tented marketplaces, grooves cut out of the side of the wall meant solely for people to sleep. It wasn't the best of places, but it offered people a home and a place to belong when society no longer welcomed them.

She took the steps forward on her own. Walking past the wall and into our community, then halted. Her eyes were wide as she took in the people surrounding her. There were hundreds. Women. Children. Men. Each one forced from above ground because they no longer served a purpose after the government failed them. But here they thrived. The community was one and helping each other was not a sign of the weakness the corrupt city above viewed it as.

She turned around, looking at all of us. "This is impossible."

She didn't even register that Warren's hand was on her hip as he pulled her closer and leaned down to her ear. "Nothing is impossible."

"Why?" she breathed.

"Because we aren't welcome up there." He pointed out.

Her eyes raked over us. "No one would know by looking at you that you're different. Not a single person top side would have turned a head toward you."

Though that may be true for the three of us while we walked around fully clothed, that was not the case without the material to shield. At least for Ansel and me. There was no hiding the scales that shimmered over my chest and thighs. And for Ansel, though he can pretend he is semi-normal as he clicked his tongue to locate objects as he walked, it wasn't the case when he hid thick wings under his clothing.

"You'd think, wouldn't you? Unless you're different and even your own family treats you so. Some of us have been lucky, I won't deny that. But there are so many of us who grew into a world that wanted nothing to do with their differences. Tell me, the first time you wrapped the shadow around your body and hid from the human eyes, what did your parents say?"

She blinked a few times. "My mother loved me."

"Well then?" Warren prompted, knowing there was more to the story.

"She was kidnapped." She stated, and it was unfair and cruel, but the world had fallen into despair and everyone capable of saving it had turned a blind eye until it escalated past the point of salvation.

"Why do you think that was?" Warren questioned, and I knew she hated to think about it. I could feel the dismay radiating off her. But he had a point. Those in command had failed us all and fuck, it was up to us to fix it.

Tiny fingers rubbed against my leg and when I looked down, I saw nothing. I smiled. Counting to five slowly before whipping myself around as fast as I could, catching sight of the little girl. Speed. She was so damn fast it was like a blur. She giggled as I narrowed my eyes at her, putting my hands on my hip in false indignation. Still, my chest purred slightly, the rumble of joy impossible to hide.

Gia giggled before looking around me, spotting Doe. With a blink, she was back at my legs, her little hands wrapping around my thighs as she hid herself behind me. I looked up. Doe was watching us curiously and I'm sure she would have tons of questions, but I was terrified to answer her. The people in this community were almost sacred to me, and any threat to them put me into fight mode.

I licked my lips and looked down at the little girl. "Gia, don't be rude to our guest."

Her enormous eyes looked at Doe, widening by the second before she whispered. "Omega."

Like everyone else here, Gia was created. The government never failed to admit they were wrong until they were too wrong to deny it any longer. I nodded my head once at Gia. "Omega."

She looked on in awe, fascinated at the woman who stood before us, closer to Warren than I think she even realized. I tried to fight the smile. Our omega was warming up well to us. I cleared my throat. "Doe, this is Gia. Gia, would you like to show her around?"

The little girl's chest puffed up proudly, finding the honor of helping the omega. Her fingers released from my denim-clad legs, and she stepped out from behind me. Wordlessly, she went to Doe and grabbed her fingers, pulling her forward. Doe went willingly and right behind her was Warren, not willing to let an inch of space be between them.

I knew through all his façade he feared she would run, and he was already so infatuated. But where would she run to, would be the real question? She was like us, a loner to her core. The whole evening and day that I kept watch outside her window, she received not a single phone call. She made none either. She didn't watch television, hell she didn't even own one. She ate a cheese sandwich. Drank a little water and way too much coffee. Slept. And when she wasn't doing any of those things, she poured herself into reading our files repeatedly, nonstop, for hours. I wonder if she had the tiny mole by my right eye memorized by now. Did it show in the image? If it did, I knew she could locate it with her eyes closed.

Gia led Doe deeper into our man-made city and Doe couldn't help but slow down to take it all in. People stopped and stared. Their mouths hanging open as the slightly breathless word, "omega", fell from their lips. She didn't realize what a miracle she was. The rumors had been true, after all. Years of research and reading about biological urges and reproductions of various species had led us to a conclusion, and that conclusion had been correct. An omega existed and now that she was here, it wasn't just us who could identify her. Every person in this room knew who and what she was, and she could deny it all she wanted, but the truth was inescapable.

After traveling through the rows of one-room homes, and through the small marketplace, she turned, her eyes wide. "You built this." It wasn't a question. She knew.

"I want more for them than this." Warren's eyes burned into her as he took a step closer.

"If we just talk to the government, we can find a better solution." she stated.

And damn it, she was so naïve in her confidence. She had no clue that the government was using her for their own gain. And they would continue to use her until she wised up and realized that her world was filled with deception. Then? Well, then they would come for her too.

"No." His words were harsh as he pulled her close, his eyes looking down at her with adoration and a bit of worry. "If we tell them, they come for us."

I saw her weakening the longer they stared at each other and the tension between them was so thick I could feel the pulse of it against my skin. "They will destroy us."

Warren leaned down, not caring to ask as he buried his nose into her neck. He wanted to be tough, and hell, he was the toughest, most terrifying man I knew. But around this woman, he was weak, and a weakness of this magnitude could be bad if this didn't go his way. She closed her eyes against his nuzzling, letting him rub his scent against her, though I doubt she even realized that's what he was doing.

With a final inhale, she muttered, "You're aware I'm armed."

Did she realize her fingers were playing with his hair even as she issued a subtle threat? "It only makes me harder when I think about it." He muttered the words against her skin before he licked her neck. Before she reacted to him, she pulled away. "Gia, why don't you take our Doe to get something to eat? I think she's hungry."

He couldn't help it. He was already trying to take care of her even before she promised to stay. The little girl's fingers wrapped around Doe's again, and together they walked down our self-made street to a giant mess hall area we had created. Doe looked over her shoulder and smiled at us, before turning her back.

"I will have her." Warren muttered when she was just out of ear shot. "And I'll kill anyone who tries to stop me."

CHAPTER
Seven

THEA

The best food I've eaten in my life. The absolute best. I don't really cook, which I would not admit out loud. But this plate of spaghetti, handmade by the sweet little Gia's mom, had to be the simplest and most delicious thing in existence. It beat my cheese sandwiches any day. This alone made me want to never go topside again. Almost.

I toyed with the beads around my neck, a gift from one woman, Leah. Hand crafted and sold through venders that never once realized a mutant made their merchandise. They had Warren to thank for that. As annoying as he was, he did them well down here, taking care of everything he could to make their lives easier.

"Do you like the food?" Warren watched me intently while Rex damn near laid in my lap. Such an odd bunch, for sure.

"You know I do." He smirked. "It's my second plate."

I normally didn't eat this much, but when Leah came back and scooped a second helping, I absolutely would not tell her no. "You could use a few extra pounds."

I glared. "Absolutely not. I can't do my job with a thick waist."

"You don't need to do your job." His brows furrowed.

"Had you missed the part where I'm a single girl paying bills and living the solo life?" I absolutely could not let the rent slip.

"Single?" Warren looked so offended that I wanted to smooth the lines by his eyes. "You're mine."

"You can't just declare something and make it true." I pointed out, but the way his mouth growled *mine* had my lower region disagreeing.

He leaned forward. "A declaration of ownership needs actions. Is that what you want?"

"No." No, please. I didn't think I'd be able to reject any actions he put forth. "Tonight has been fun in its own weird way. But you're still my mark and I still have a job to do and if you're so worried about the people here, I can talk to my contacts. I can let them know about you and see what …"

A hand was around my throat, squeezing it tightly, cutting off my words. Warren had leaned across the table, his face in mine as anger rippled through him and for the first time, I felt threatened. Gone was the man who flirted shamelessly and in his place was the fearless monster who had no problem mutating and murdering those who stumbled in his path.

"You will say nothing."

I wish I could speak or try to reword my thoughts, but my mind was cloudy, and my words refused to come out.

"These are my people. My family." He seethed. "I will not have you put them in danger because you think you know more than us about living the life of the rejected. Do you understand me?" I opened my mouth, but nothing came out. Grey spots danced in my vision as he flexed his fingers in his impossibly powerful grip. I wanted to answer him. I did. But never in my life had I felt such immense fear while also having my core heat with desire. "Nod your head."

His order had me frantically nodding. A slow, sinister smile tugged at his lips until it formed a full grin. "Good. Very good little Doe."

His fingers released my throat and I gasped for air for two full seconds before he crashed his lips to my own. The contrast of lack of oxygen and his lips set my body on fire, my skin instantly igniting with pins and needles prickling every surface. And he didn't let up, didn't release me from the trance his lips put on me as he worked his mouth roughly against mine, willing me to kiss back, and fuck, I tried to resist. I really did. My mind willed me to push him away, but my body? My body wanted his tongue on me, caressing every inch.

I moved my tongue against his, my hand going up to his neck to hold him in place willingly as a finger snuck up my inner thigh. A finger? Impossible, Warren was across the table, his large body standing and bending over to devour my lips. The finger wasn't his, but the vibration coming from Rex let me know he was past the point of enjoying this interaction. Rex's fingers danced against the denim of my jeans, applying pressure to my core. And what was wrong with me?

I was kissing Warren with lungs that burned with need for air and I couldn't help my body from riding against Rex's digits as I sought pleasure. I needed away from these men; I needed a break from the unnatural feeling that I belonged here, when I clearly had different morals than any of this group. My hand went to Rex's wrist, stopping his movement before my other hand went to Warren, pushing him back.

The minute his lips left mine, I gasped for air, the oxygen filling my lungs and soothing the scorch. "I can't do this."

"Do what?" he seemed genuinely confused and hell, I wanted to close the short distance between us and begin a new assault, capturing his swollen lips with my own and showing him who was really in control of the situation.

"I'd like to go home now." I stated.

"You assume it's that easy." He stared blankly.

In a flash, I had a knife in my hand, holding it to his chest. It was a false threat, and I didn't even fool myself with thinking he believed it was anything but. I just needed him to know that he didn't always have the upper hand. He may be the most powerful man among these people, but I was not under his thumb. I wielded my power and never would I hand over the reins.

"I don't assume. Take me home or I'll find a way myself."

"Are you going to stab me? I beg you to do so." God, he was so fucked up in the head.

"I'm asking you nicely. Take me home."

It became a stare off, Warren and I each so intense and neither of us willing to be the first to blink. He didn't want me to leave, but staying here wasn't what I had agreed upon. Hell, I didn't know what I had agreed upon. I surely didn't agree to like their infuriating company, or to be amazed by what they have going on. I didn't agree to liking the meal or to fucking crave their touch either. I agreed to nothing, really, and that fact was throwing me off kilter.

Ansel's arm cut in between us as he pushed Warren back. "I'll take her home."

Warren didn't even glance in his direction. "You will not breathe a word of this place to anyone on the outside. My goal was to make you see the world differently, not have you bring a threat to our doorstep."

Didn't he see the opportunity that even the mention of something more for them could bring? He was blinded by his hate, but I'd lurked in the shadows long enough to know that the government strived on inclusion, not exclusion, and my position only proved it to be true. "I can't promise I won't ask questions."

"As long as those questions don't endanger us." His eyes burned so intently I struggled to not look away. For a moment

I swore I saw fire, a slight shimmer of red and orange wave under the surface of his skin.

"Do you think so little of me that I would put your people in danger just to prove a point?" I questioned.

"I think they sent you to kill us, and tons of innocent mutants before us." He pushed and challenged me, and that fact made me uncomfortable. "But I'd like to think you wouldn't harm me." Without a second's hesitation, his lips crushed to mine again, the kiss bruising and swift before he pulled away and looked toward Ansel. "Take her home."

He was gone, not bothering to look back after that, not even a goodbye before he disappeared. I fought the jumble of words inside of me, wishing I knew what to say to the men who sat beside me. After the silence grew uncomfortably heavy, Rex spoke. "It won't be the end, little Doe."

Then he pushed up and was gone. I turned to Ansel, clearly aware that he could not see me, and waited for him to speak. He didn't. He just pushed himself up from the table and walked, assuming I would follow him. I did. I had no other choice. He was leading me to the surface, a place that could take ages to find on my own, even knowing the tunnels.

Walking through their self-made streets, past the curious eyes and sheltered faces, I wondered how much of what Warren said was true. Sure, he believed it. Everyone always believes in their own cause. But was it true? The sorrowed looks I got, made me want to believe every word he spouted. In the dark tunnels of the underground, below the city that once never slept, I felt the very shadows I controlled push against me, trying to grab at my skin and demand I comfort myself as I blanketed them around me.

He wouldn't know. The surrounding darkness is all he knows. But it seemed morally wrong to hide myself when he was right next to me, clicking his tongue as he searched for directions and objects. "Were you always blind?"

Shit, that was rude of me. Wasn't it? Still, he didn't hesitate to answer. "I got my shot at four. Sometimes, if I allow myself to relax long enough, I still can remember what colors looked like."

I couldn't imagine how heartbreaking it would be to know colors, then know nothing. I played with the shadows from an early age in my life. My life wasn't ever altered so drastically. "What was your favorite?"

"Yellow." I saw him smile at the thought. "It's a color we take advantage of. One so often dismissed."

I didn't know what to say to that. Something about the way he admitted that made my chest ache. "My favorite color is purple."

My admission came without prompting, and he smirked. "A lady of blackness loves colors."

"Just because I am one with the shadows does not mean it solely defines me." I pointed out.

"Exactly."

"Exactly what?"

He stopped, his head tilted to the side. "What do you think Warren is trying to do?"

"Be a control freak." I muttered, though even I didn't really believe that.

"We are not defined by what makes us different. It is a piece of us, not all of us, but it's being used as an excuse for elimination."

"I've not seen proof of this accusation." I crossed my arms, feeling vulnerable.

"Proof? Did you see children and women being trafficked in there? I can't even see, and I know all there is in there is safety and protection." He paused. "Protection Doe. Ask all the questions in the world if you must. But ask the right questions."

Ask the right questions. I didn't know what the right questions were. I didn't know where to begin or what was a question that was far too risky to bring up. But he was right. If I really was concerned, I'd sort things out for myself. "Even if this was true, what does he want from me?"

"Besides the obvious?" He was walking again, and I was forced to follow. The clicks nearly as soothing as being close to the man.

"I don't even know what the obvious is."

"The obvious is you. He'll have you, you know. There is no question about it and when he has you, we will all have you." He crawled up a ladder before pushing open a door. I followed him up and onto the empty street.

"What's the least obvious?" I finally asked when we were eye to eye again. He looked at me, seeing everything and nothing.

"Power. You'll have the power." He blinked. "We are at your apartment complex. Would you like me to walk you up?"

I cringed, thinking about the stairs of the walkup. "I've got it. Thank you."

He turned back to the drain hole before turning back to me and kissing my forehead. "We'll be in contact, Doe." Then he disappeared.

I stood there in the night, confused. It wasn't until I entered my apartment and checked all the securities that realization hit me. Ansel didn't say Warren wanted power. He said *you*. As in me. *You'll have the power*. Only I had no fucking clue what power he was talking about.

CHAPTER
Eight

WARREN

The taste of her still lingered on my tongue and I wanted nothing more than to storm after her, throw her over my shoulders and drag her back to my private space, show her exactly all the reasons she should stay with us, let her feel the importance her mere existence has.

But I didn't.

The memory of her throat contracting against my palm gave me the power to walk away because I liked her submission too fucking much to stay. I pushed down the savagery inside of me, begging myself to keep control and not take her on the table in the middle of our damn mess hall. My cock was so fucking hard, despite her defiance and the possible jeopardy she put us in, that I could barely walk away.

"Want me to watch her?" Rex broke the surrounding silence a few minutes later when he found me in my office.

Everything in me wanted to send him after her, protect her, watch her, make sure she was a hundred percent trustworthy, but I couldn't do that. I trusted my gut this time and hoped it didn't steer me wrong. "I'll go to her tomorrow. There is nothing she is planning to do tonight. Of that, I'm sure."

He seemed unsure when he asked, "Do you think she'll come back?"

"How can she not? You've seen us?" I joked light heartedly, but I wanted more than anything for the omega to come willingly to us. But if she didn't, I'd take her by force, whatever means necessary. I'm giving her the illusion of being the good guy at the moment, but that illusion only lasts as long as her compliance does. If I had to, I'd take what's mine and I would not regret a single bit of it even as she pounded against my chest, begging me to let her be free.

The only free she can ever truly be is when she was near us. That isn't an assumption, that's just a fact. The government would never allow her the freedom she so clearly needs, the freedom to be who she was without using her ability to hide from the world, unless she takes it. And well, we will be right there beside her, taking it for everyone else who isn't brave enough to do so.

"What's your plan?" Rex saw past the insecurity I had that maybe she wouldn't pick us and cut straight to the heart of it.

"I'm already itching to be close." I admitted.

"Then why did you let her go?" His eyes burned into me, and I had to look down at the papers I was working on to avoid his heavy gaze.

"I had to."

"Her picking us and us picking her do not have to align. You hadn't gotten this powerful by chance, Warren. Take what we want, and I'll help deal with the consequences later."

Oh, my boys wanted her badly, too. Why did the thought make me hard? Then again, everything about her had that effect on me. Her smell, her sass, the way her waist dipped in, and her hips flared out. I liked the feel of them under my fingertips, though she was unaware each time I snuck my hands onto her body.

"I want her to choose."

"How long will you wait?" He picked up a pencil and twirled it.

"As long as I need."

Lie. I was already ready to barrel after her and take what was mine, claim her, bury my scent so deep into her body that there was no thought or question over who owned her. She would scream my name, pant it, beg for more and fuck me. Wouldn't that be the most satisfying pleasure to my soul?

"Are you going to tell her?" He dropped the pencil and bent to grab it, his long frame disappearing from my sight for a moment.

"Our plans? No. Not yet. Not until I know she is ours."

Rex's head nodded his approval. "I figured that was the plan."

"Get some rest. I want your eyes on her first thing in the morning." I ordered, and he nodded and stood, tossing the pencil back on my desk before he strolled out.

Turns out, having Rex keep eyes on her wasn't the worst decision I'd made. By noon, she was already leaving her apartment. He followed her, his body blending in perfectly with the surroundings. Did she realize what a perfect pair they made? His ability to blend with her ability to disappear, was the perfect pairing for what I needed. She would fit in flawlessly with our bunch, if only she would see that.

He followed her to a pub, where he sat and watched her for me. Meanwhile, I had no issue meeting her back at her place. I'd been without her long enough. I'd missed her scent being close to me and though I know it wasn't the truth, at least not yet, I felt like her scent was fading from my memory. My body yearned to be close, and I couldn't help but wonder, if she gave into our lust instead of fighting it, how explosive would that be?

I didn't bother with the door. It was too risky and if what Rex had told me was true, that she had so many locks on the door it would be nearly impossible to merely pick the locks and let myself in. The windows were locked, but as I traveled along her building, watching the inside of her minimalistic living space, I saw a crawl space. If her apartment had a crawlspace, I was positive that so did another. The building was old, a walk-up that had to be sitting here in despair long before the shift in government's control and things started falling in disarray.

I hopped from fire escapes to ledges, making my way around the whole fucking building until I found a single room on the opposite side of the building with a crawlspace entrance. The window was unlocked, fucking lucky for me, not so lucky for them. Humans. They don't fucking care about safety and they should, especially in the new world we live in where police are corrupt as they come and not a single eye turned in the direction as a person is murdered on a busy street.

It was vile what this world had become. Disgusting. Heartbreaking. And I wish I could say I'd been doing my part to make it better, but that was a lie. I did my part to improve my world, to make the world of my people better. Humans, I couldn't care less about. Sure, I didn't go out of my way to take their life, but if they stepped foot in my path, I'd do what I had to. They created this divided world, now they had to live with the consequences of living in it. And if the argument came, where they claimed this was never the world they wanted and they didn't approve, the falsity of it would only drive my rage further. Because if no one stepped up against the inhumanity of it all for fear that their way of living would change, they were just as guilty of the sins that were committed.

The window shimmied upward, the pane stalling and sticking in the swollen and weathered wooden tracks. The track making a god-awful squeak as I pushed the window upward. I hoped and prayed to whatever god, if they existed, that no one heard the window. The prayers went unanswered. Just as I had got my leg in the door, a woman walked into the room. Her scream echoed through the apartment when she set eyes on me and I froze, then she froze as we looked into each other's eyes.

"I just want to use the crawlspace." I thought it was a reasonable request. I didn't want to attack her. I didn't want to kill her. I just wanted access to the door.

I heard her heartbeat pick up, the thrum of it rapid as she searched her pockets. "I'm calling the police."

"Ma'am, there is no use getting them involved." I held my hands out as I tried to calm her.

"I will not have my home tainted by your presence. The people like you, it's what's wrong with this world."

Like me? A mutant? A man? A seemingly criminal? I wasn't sure which she was referring to, but I knew that when her fingers hit the button of her phone to unlock it, she had sealed her own fate. I opened my mouth, my soul pulling and calling to her as I sucked her life from her body. It came so willingly, the weak human, floating from her body to my own, feeding my energy and fueling me. It slid down my throat and not once did her soul fight it. It wanted to leave. It wanted death. It enjoyed the process.

Her body fell limply to the ground and odds were, they would declare her dead by natural causes, but there was nothing natural about your soul being sucked from your body. It hurt so badly that you open your mouth to scream, but no scream can escape you. Each strand that is attached within you breaks, feeling like a thousand knives all at once, and one by one, as the strands break, the soul pulls away until there is nothing anchoring it to your life and your life just ceases to exist. Your heart stops. Your blood stops flowing. And even as this is happening, you're aware, so fucking aware, of a process you cannot stop.

It fuels me. Fuels the fire and the beast within. They made a mistake when changing me, forcing too much of their serum onto my little body just to see if I'd survive. I survived. But what they created wasn't merely a mutant. It was the definition of mutation. It altered my DNA, changing the structure of my being and creating a monster like they had never seen before. But this monster would no longer hide from the world, not with the little Doe at my side, and I could not wait to release it.

My foot kicked into the body as I finished climbing into the room. It was a small space, barely large enough to be a closet, but was classified in this city as a room because, well, it had a door that opened and closed. Real estate space was at its prime and it didn't matter if you could sleep in a room. It counted when trying to sell the space to a client.

Without giving the woman another thought, I reached up, pushing the door to the space away from the opening until I could heave myself up through the hole. It was effortless really, and after replacing the crawlspace door, I was at the other side of the building in minutes, my body directly over the door that was part of Doe's space. I could smell her scent all over, just from the nearness of her living quarters, and my cock was already pulsing.

Fuck, I wanted her.

I would own her.

I'd fuck her so hard she never had doubts about that.

I slid the crawlspace door to the side and shimmied myself down into her apartment before adjusting the door one more time. I wondered, was she as in-tuned to me as I was to her? Did her smell work as well as ours, labeling me as her alpha? Denial. There were so many things she was in denial about, but this, this was a hundred percent unavoidable. She would never be rid of us now.

The sound of keys jingled at the front door as a text came through from Rex.

She's home.

Like a lovesick sap, I smiled down at the phone, my heart pounding and my palms sweating at the thought of seeing her again.

Go home. I'll meet you there later. I texted back. I could handle the girl perfectly fine on my own, and he'd been trailing her for hours.

Copy that, boss.

I shoved the phone into my pants pocket and waited. She would find me, this I knew. How she would react would be the real question. The front door slammed, followed by a chorus of locks as they clicked into place. Jesus, she really went overboard on the locks and look at me, still in here. I heard her footsteps as they traveled through the place, listened as she jiggled each window.

Her steps grew closer. My stomach tightened. The scent traveling off her body was so strong I couldn't help but react.

I barely registered her in my view before a knife sailed through the room, barely missing my ear. I jumped. Me. I fucking jumped because never in my life had I been caught so fucking off guard than I was with this girl. How the hell she even got a knife that close to me was a mystery. Fuck. She was a danger.

She already had another dagger in her hand. "Next time I won't miss. How the fuck did you get in here?" I loved when she talked dirty to me. I let my eyes travel upward toward the crawlspace door and she cursed again. "I knew that was going to cause me trouble one day. Get out!"

"I think I'll stay, little Doe." I cooed.

"That wasn't a fucking option that I gave you. Fuck. I knew I should have trusted my gut. I swore I sensed Rex by me today." She stepped closer, holding the knife toward me. "I didn't give you permission to stalk me."

"Funny thing about the habit of stalking, permission is rarely given." I looked down at the knife before taking a step forward toward it. "You must have known you never truly would be free of us, didn't you? You would have to kill us first. Are you going to kill us, little Doe? Are you going to start with me?"

I took another step forward, taunting her with my fearlessness. She didn't move, her body frozen. Her heart beating so loud I could hear it radiating through the room. Her blood swooshed through her veins. Her soul... it sang to me like a siren bringing in ships to their doom. Her beauty, as captivating as medusa, though I knew for a fact, her bite was just as damaging. But I'd gladly let her be my medusa. I'd fall victim to her beauty and let her turn me to stone if she promised to never take the intensity of her stare away from my motionless body.

Then the surrounding silence broke, the tension snapped, and somehow, my lips were on hers, biting and begging and praying to whatever gods were out there to let me keep her. Her back hit the wall, her fingers tearing at my shirt. My hands? They were everywhere. Grabbing and tugging, thankful that she had on a tasteful skirt today instead of the damn cargo pants.

I ran my fingers up her legs, feeling the soft give of her skin that encased the hard muscles of her body. My lips sunk into hers before leaving them to devour and mark the skin at her neck. I was too far gone in lust, too fucking willing to lay her down right here, that I nearly missed the knife at my neck. I blinked. If she thought that would deter me, she was wrong. Still, I gave her space, allowing her to push me away.

Her lips were swollen and red, her chin carrying a slight pink look from the scruff of my facial hair. "We need to talk."

She made the demand as the knife pushed into my skin, barely avoiding piercing it. "We're talking."

I swallowed hard and tilted my head, trying to force her to prick my skin, but she pulled back slightly. "I talked to an acquaintance."

I felt fury coil inside of me. "The fuck you did!"

She held out her hand to calm me. "Listen, I didn't tell them about you. I just asked questions."

Only that didn't make me feel any better. Questions piqued interest in their path to find answers. "What type of questions?"

She looked down, her face turned red with embarrassment before she met my eyes again. In the light, they didn't glow nearly as vibrant. They almost seemed normal. "I - You were right. I mean, I think."

And fuck, if that admission didn't have me slamming into the door with my hips pinning her down as I devoured every inch of her fucking hot mouth. I was right. She fucking said the words and she couldn't take it back now. I was right.

CHAPTER
Nine

THEA

I asked all the right questions, at least I thought I did. But the answers unsettled me because deep down, I knew what Warren had been telling me was the truth and I didn't want to admit it. It started way before the oversight of not putting their crime in their files. It was little things here and there, tiny little details that if I let myself examine too much, I would have known the truth. But I wasn't ready for the truth then. Hell, I'm barely ready for the truth now.

But when I put on my black pencil skirt and planned to have a few afternoon drinks with an acquaintance from work, I forced myself to be ready for all the answers. But I wasn't, not really. I wasn't ready for how aversive a person I thought was my friend would become. Or how many answers he did not answer to the best of his capability. The answers made me uneasy and when I left there, I felt like my very own skin was crawling.

"Do you find the government's treatment of mutants fair?"
"Relatively."

"Do you think we should eliminate them?"

"Don't you?"

"Given the current tension between mutants and humans, do you think the government is using us to target them?"

"Come on, Thea. Don't be dense."

But he didn't know the truth. He didn't know I was just like them. No one did, really. At least, I didn't think so.

"If a mutant walked into the bar."

I had set it up like a bad joke, only I never finished or got to any sort of punchline. *"I'd kill him on the spot."*

The entire conversation made my stomach sour, yet I pushed on through the visit, thinking maybe it was me and not him. Maybe I was putting too much thought into it. Maybe Warren had gotten under my skin and into my head and I'd believe anything he said because when he looked at me, I felt like I had more worth than I'd ever had in this single lifetime.

The final nail came when he leaned in and asked if I heard about the latest assignments going out. An elimination of level three mutants. Level three. Anyone who had a visible mutation. I tried to control the pitch in my stomach, realizing that in the five seconds of first meeting Rex, I could determine he was a level three. A visual representation of the mutation gene. If Ansel removed his clothes, I didn't doubt that he too fell under that category. And Warren? Fuck, but he was the biggest wildcard.

The thought that the government actively sought the execution of them based on appearance and not on what they've done was disgusting. But I held that thought inside, not willing to voice it, and when the meeting was over, I literally could not leave soon enough. I didn't know what I wanted to do with the information that had been slipped to me. I didn't even know if I wanted anything to do with Warren and his men, but damn if they didn't make me feel safe in this fucked up world of uncertainty... But I also was no damsel. I didn't need a knight to protect me from the harm of this world. I could protect myself.

Though, a knight would sure be fucking nice sometimes.

My legs ached walking up the flights of stairs to my apartment and I made a mental note to one day find a place that offered an elevator option because these stairs were killer on the thighs. After placing my keys in the locks of my apartment, I opened the door, stepped in, and shut it. Instantly, I could smell him. The scent of Warren wafted lightly through my apartment and my body froze before continuing locking the door.

He wasn't here? Was he? It was impossible.

I walked into my kitchen, palming the knife in my hand just in case. He was all nice and fun last night, but I wouldn't put it past any of them to show up for a murder session. After all, I've seen photos of what they could do and fuck, I didn't want to be one of them. Traveling through my apartment, I checked each window, shaking them to make sure that the locks hadn't been tampered. They hadn't. But the closer I got to the hall, the smell grew, and I knew, I fucking knew, he was back there.

I squeezed my palm around the handle of the knife, preparing myself. And when I turned the corner, when I turned into the small bedroom toward the back of my apartment and saw his handsome face, I did not hesitate to send the knife flying. I didn't want to hit him, though I could have. I should have, honestly.

"Next time I won't miss. How the fuck did you get in here?" He smirked, not even looking phased by the dagger that could have killed him. His eyes travelled upward, locking on for a moment to the stupid crawl space door. Fuck. "I knew that was going to cause me trouble one day. Get out!"

"I think I'll stay, little Doe." He stated confidently and hell if his smug look wasn't cute.

"That wasn't a fucking option that I gave you. Fuck. I knew I should have trusted my gut. I swore I sensed Rex by me today." I stepped closer, holding the knife toward him. "I didn't give you permission to stalk me."

"Funny thing about the habit of stalking, permission is rarely given." He looked down at the knife before taking a step forward toward it. The psychopath wanted me to pierce his skin and I wouldn't give him the pleasure of it. "You must have known you never truly would be free of us, didn't you? You would have to kill us first. Are you going to kill us, little Doe? Are you going to start with me?"

He took a step forward, stepping toward the knife I held instead of away and he was a fucking masterpiece. I wanted to reach out, rub my finger over the faint scar that slashed into his brow, and figure out all the mysteries that surrounded him. My heart pounded. My soul felt like it was screaming at his nearness. The haphazard reaction was because of this one man standing in front of me, daring me to end his life.

I'm not sure who moved first, but I'd like to think I wasn't nearly as weak as he was. Our lips crashed together, our teeth clinking as we tore at each other's mouths. His hands found my thighs and before I could blink, he had my back hitting the wall, his fingers skimming my bare skin. Fuck, it felt like his mouth knew my own, his body perfectly in sync. I was drowning, gasping, clenching my fingers into his clothes and begging for more.

Begging. And I couldn't beg. Not to him. Not for more.

I pushed through the ecstasy of his body against mine and as his lips traveled to my neck, I pulled my knife up to his throat. He took longer than he should have, but slowly he pulled away, taking step back so that I could breathe.

He eyed me hungrily, his chest heaving as I spoke. "We need to talk."

I pushed the knife deeper into his skin, the slight give into the softness of his flesh reminding me I was in control, even as he spoke carelessly. "We're talking."

He tilted his neck toward the knife, trying to force me to pierce his skin, and I couldn't. I'd killed a hundred times, but I couldn't bring myself to break his skin with the blade. "I talked to an acquaintance."

Anger lit his eyes. "The fuck you did!"

I held out my hand to calm his fury. "Listen, I didn't tell them about you. I just asked questions."

Only that didn't make him feel any better. His brows furrowed, and I wanted to reach forward to smooth the crease in between them. He was a criminal, I tried to remind myself, but the reminder was pointless. "What type of questions?"

I looked down, finding it hard to meet his eyes, knowing how triumphant he would be by the statement I was about to make. I didn't imagine he was a man who let you admit you were wrong without a healthy dose of gloating. "I - You were right. I mean, I think."

He moved so fucking quickly, I hadn't even realized he budged until I was slammed against the door, his mouth on my lips with his hard cock pinning me to the door of the room. I let the kiss consume me, felt it course through my body like electricity. And fuck, even with the knife I still held in my hand, he didn't hesitate as he pushed his body into my own. I pushed him back, forcing him into the hallway without breaking our lips' contact.

Fuck.

I should stop. I wanted to, didn't I? Sex with Warren couldn't be anything but toxic, and toxic was bad.

It was bad unless it came as one very large man with a very large cock who wasn't afraid to get his throat slit.

I moaned into his mouth, my fingers finding his belt buckle and working it clumsily as his own fingers worked the buttons on my shirt. The knife in my hand nicked against his thigh as his pants fell and his cock jumped. "Psychopath."

I breathed the word against his lips and felt him smile, before he picked me up and turned me, hitting my body hard against the wall, making a picture fall to the floor. He didn't bother removing an article of clothing, not after he abandoned the buttons of the shirt in leu of tearing it open to get to my breasts. His fingers traveled up my thigh, not caring as he tore off my panties.

"I'm going to make you scream so fucking loud, the neighbors will come." He threatened and though I doubted that fact to be true, my core still pulsed with the promise.

"Don't make promises you can't fucking keep." I growled before his lips crushed into mine again.

With a single flex of his hip and bruising hands on my legs, he pushed himself inside of me and I swear, I nearly fainted. His cock felt like it was made for me, the stretch so damn delicious that if he moved, I doubted I would survive the pleasure of it. His body stiffened, his mouth broke from mine as his chest heaved, his breath coming out in pants.

"You fit around me like a fucking glove." He growled before his hip flexed, pushing his cock deeper into my body.

My nails scratched into him, sinking so deep into his skin that I heard a growl. I wiggled my body against him, begging him to move inside of me because without the movement I couldn't take his size. I felt too full. It was too much. I could hardly handle it. My eyes watered, I couldn't take in air and all I wanted was to feel the stroke of my nerves as they ignited into the flames I knew Warren would bring.

He pulled his cock out, slamming back into me with such force the wall behind me cracked. It didn't deter him, not that I thought it would. A man like Warren strived on the power he held, and I knew he wouldn't even slow until he made a point. His hips moved fast, his body hard as he moved me around, slamming into furniture as our connected bodies fought each other. I'd win in the end, I had no doubt about it. But reaching the finish line had never been so fun.

I should have stopped this before it got this far. He was a mark, the man they sent me to kill two days ago. And now? Now he worked himself so roughly into my body that I was losing the battle of hate and adoration. I despised him on principle, but my soul craved the feeling he ignited in my every cell. It shouldn't be this easy to be fucked by him, I should have put up a bigger fight, but as he turned my body around, and pushed my head in the single armchair I owned, forcing my body to bend as he slammed back into me, I was positive if I'd had a longer fight against this pull, it would have only been my own form of self-punishment.

A moan slipped out of my lips as his hand bruised into my hips. His palm rested against my back. I should have felt shameful, like a wanton hussy, but as his dirty words fell from his lips, words of need and murmurs of praise, all I felt was power. His fingers traveled up my back, reaching for my hair before he gripped it tight, wrapping the strands around his hand and pulling me back toward him.

He captured my lip with his and the new angle set me on fire. I moaned into his mouth, biting his lips as he pulled away. "A fucking dream." His chest heaved. "No fucking doubt who owns you."

Was that a question or a declaration? I didn't fucking know. I didn't care. We all knew the truth, even if it was only momentary. "You."

His fingers tightened in my hair, causing a delicious bite of pain. "Say it like you fucking mean it, Doe."

"You." I moaned, feeling the tension inside my core build. There was no doubt I was seconds away from releasing, nearly ready to topple over the edge.

"My fucking name, Doe." He demanded and wasn't that fucking an ironic reminder that I'm currently on the brink of the most blissful fuck of my life, and he didn't even know my name. There was no value in what we were doing. I was just another fucking dime in his jar of coins. Even so, I wanted every second of it. I wanted to feel. I wanted... fuck. I didn't even know what I wanted anymore because what I thought I knew was a lie and every truth and moral I had strictly abided by was out the window when I was near this man.

I swallowed hard, his name rolling off my tongue in the most seductive of manners before panic fully set in. "Warren." He didn't see them, he didn't see the set of eyes staring at us through the window, with their guns raised for an attack. "Warren."

I spoke his name, and he groaned as he pushed hard into my body, holding me forward. "Fuck, yes."

The window broke and on reflex, I reached for my knife inches from my hand, snatching it up and flinging it at the intruder without a moment's hesitation. The intruder's gun fell to the floor and inside me, Warren exploded, his cum pulsing in spurts inside of me as a ball swelled, pressing up against the nerves of my inner wall. I screamed as pleasure hit me hard, fighting the panic as another body entered.

"You fucking killed a man for me, Doe." He panted, the words triggering another wave of cum from him.

"Did you…"

"I can't fucking help it. It was hot." He growled as I reached into the sleeve of my shirt for the holster there. Riding the waves of pleasure while killing a man was new to me, still... I fucking couldn't help the sounds that were tearing from my throat as my fingers frantically searched for a spare knife. I found the knife as my pleasure peeked, not able to open my eyes as I flung it forward.

I heard it hit its mark before a body fell with a sickening thud to the floor. When my orgasm faded some and I was able, I opened my eyes seeing the man with a knife in his head, laying on top of his friend. "You need to pull out."

He needed to pull out.

We needed to get out.

This was a bad sign.

I recognized the logo on their clothes, and I knew for a fact that I no longer was safe. I raised too many questions to someone I viewed as the closest person to a friend that I had at work, and it went badly, so fucking badly.

"I can't." Warren groaned and when I looked back at him, his head was tilted back, and his eyes were fluttering.

"What the fuck do you mean, you can't?" I growled and his cock jumped.

"Until my hard-on fades little Doe, I'm stuck inside of you. The knot on my cock won't allow me to pull out."

"Excuse me?" I nearly panicked at his declaration. "I don't even know what the fuck you're talking about."

"We've been trying to tell you." Another pulse of the ball inside of me sent a wave through my body and I gasped. "Fuck, you're so fucking mine. No denying it."

It pulsed again and this time, I couldn't stop the second orgasm that tore through me or the scream as I clawed my fingers into the chair, trying to gain hold on anything to help me ride through the pleasure. "Fuck you, Warren."

I screamed the words, angry that he had an apparent magic cock that could make me come so fucking hard and so damn easily. "I could go again."

Was he fucking serious? We just got attacked while he was balls deep in my pussy and all he could think of was another round. Hell, another round with him might kill me. I can already feel my body bruising and aching from being manhandled by his large hands and demanding personality. My core squeezed around him, and he wheezed.

"Seriously. I can't fucking pull out if I'm turned on like this," I heard him swallow hard. "Don't do that again."

As if his words were pulling a trigger, my core cinched around him one more time, sending a quick wave through me. "I can't help it."

A crash from down the hall informed me we were out of time and out of time was not good when you were stuck in this position. If he couldn't pull out until he was soft, then I was determined to make him that way.

"Dead cats. Rats. Food poisoning." I muttered.

"What are you doing?" Fuck, I felt so fucking full with him inside of me. I would miss it when he left, though I couldn't voice that to him.

"Trying to kill the hard on."

There was a pause before another crash happened. Jesus, I take it they didn't pick the crawl space like Warren had. "Faster."

"Warts. Fish guts. Rotten vegetables. A grandma." His cock jumped at the last one. "Warren."

"What? I just...I'm sorry." He didn't even try to explain. Instead, he held onto my back, not fully soft but softer, and pulled away from my body slowly. He was right, it was fucking painful with him still erect, but we had no other choice. My shirt just fell back into place when my colleague appeared.

"Thea."

He called my name, but I knew it was a distraction tactic. They had trained me alongside of him. I slid across the floor, pulling the knife from the body, and flung it at him, landing the blade in the eye socket. He hit the floor hard, the angle and the weight of him jamming the blade further into his head as he fell face first into the ground that the knife protruded out the back of his skull.

I stood, frozen, looking at the body of the person I knew. Feeling numb to the entire ordeal.

"Thea." My name coming from Warren's lips had me turning. It was weird hearing him say it even when I knew everything about this situation was too fucking wrong. I stood, my hands shaking, and I would like to say that was from the orgasms, but the betrayal was setting in and I was hurt. I had risked my life for these people, for the United government, and in return they sent teams to kill me.

"Thea, we need to leave, Doe. They will send more." Warren's words barely registered in mind as I stared at him. His eyes grew wide as he stared behind me. "Thea!"

Then his mouth opened wide, his face shifted from man to a full skeleton as he inhaled. If I wasn't so terrified, I would have missed it. A single blink and the very second a faint aura slid into his mouth would have been missed. But I was so fucking confused by what I saw I didn't dare risk closing my eyes, even if it was a split second.

His lips closed the same moment the body of the man slumped backward, hitting into the cracked wall. His face morphed again, changing back to a man. And I swear I was going crazy because there was no fucking way I saw that. Another thump from the back room and Warren was in front of me, tossing me over his shoulder before taking the steps to the front door. A single pull broke all the locks and in seconds, we were on the move.

CHAPTER
Ten

ANSEL

I got a call from Rex and though Warren had ordered him to go home, he refused to follow orders and waited. It was a wise choice to trust his gut, knowing that something was off. No sooner did Doe enter the building that suspicious activity gathered. I'd like to think it was the girl. Chaos gathering around her and blanketing her like the shadows. But the suspicious activity Rex reported seemed to be more of the government type.

She didn't believe us when we told her the government was after us, but I had a sneaking suspicion she would swiftly find out.

I met Rex in minutes, already lingering in the area, just in case I was needed. I got nervous when both Warren and Rex were on a job, nervous to be left without my eyes and my partners. We were a unit, so perfectly formed that when separated, our function wasn't nearly as flawless.

My radio in my ear hit static before Rex's voice broke

through. "Half the crew is climbing the fire escape. Should we intercept?"

Rex wasn't made for the fight, not like Warren and me. His soul was far too sweet. But for the girl, I gathered he would do just about anything. I knew the feeling. It was an odd connection, the one we had with the girl. It was like from the moment her scent hit our lungs we had no other choice but to vow our services and worship the ground in front of her and though I can't see her beauty, I suspect she would be worth all the worshipping. We would devour her, every inch, like the big bad wolves coming after Red, and I hoped she ran because tracking was my specialty.

"Hello?" There was a pause. "You there, Ans?"

I spaced out, which wasn't ideal at a time like this, a time when you know in your gut that shit is about to go down and you're already prepared to stain your favorite shirt. I cleared my throat before clicking the button to talk. "Wait it out. I have no doubt that Warren and Doe can handle what's inside of there. It's outside that we need to keep in check."

We needed the eyes outside and eyes were one thing I lacked. If Rex went in, we couldn't keep track of those on the outside, and if more men came, I wouldn't be able to count numbers. I doubt they would send more men for a single girl, would they? Although, I had heard the rumors of her long before she came into our lives and maybe, just maybe, this single girl could take out ten men, and that's why the government was so damn fearful of her.

"They have six on the ground, four going up." He stated.

"Do they think she will run?" I wondered out loud because why have heavier amount on the floor when the threat is up?

"Maybe? But I don't doubt anyone who crossed their path will be handed death. She and Warren together are like walking reapers. They will have no problem getting through the team sent."

Reapers. I never thought of Warren that way, but wasn't

that what he was deep down? A reaper of souls? The face of death? But it wasn't all of who he was. He was a dual mutant, after all. And those souls he eats, they fuel his energy and strength and flame the fire that burns inside of him. If he shifted, if he pushed it that far, it would be too late for the humans. The destruction he would cause wouldn't be stopped.

We waited. Rex monitored the men outside, replaying locations as we slowly crept toward them. We wouldn't strike until necessary, but by the time we reached the point of necessity, it would be far too late for their survival.

"Fire escape is empty." Rex relayed, which meant they were on the inside.

They went in, but they would never come out. If Warren and Doe didn't do the job, we'd finish them before they stepped foot on the street. But I didn't think it would get that far. I felt the shift in the air, felt the slight tingle in the atmosphere as Warren took a soul, and I knew it would be moments before they made their way toward us.

I wasn't wrong. Two minutes later, he burst through the door and the men at the ground didn't hesitate to strike. But we were prepared, and they weren't. With a click of my tongue, I found the location of my target. Listened to the drum of the unfamiliar heartbeat before I crept behind them on silent steps. They didn't sense me until it was too late. I was not made of the shadows, but I was born to lurk in them.

My knife cut the skin at their throats like butter. As the blood pumped through the opening and trickled over my skin in spurts, the warmth reminded me of comfort and security, the reassurance of surviving another day. I held the body until the struggling stopped, holding my bloody hand over their mouth to stop the sounds from alerting the others. And when the body stopped moving, and I was sure the heart had finally stopped, I dragged the man the few feet around the corner of the building before creeping toward my next victim.

The man I approached was already in full-on combat, his strength and size being used against Rex as Rex stood between the man and Doe. I knew Doe could take him on. Hell, I could hear her struggling as she tried to free herself from Warren to do so. But she didn't need to. Not when she had us. She didn't always need to be the fighter any longer. We were a team. And as a team, it was our job to divide the work. She and Warren got the job done inside. Now it was Rex and my turn to get the job done on the outside.

Material shuffled, alerting me that Rex's arm rose as he blocked a blow of a knife. Each click of my lips told me the location of body parts, and I knew without a doubt that I would succeed. With the attacker's arm still raised, a single click and my ears could hear the location. I jammed my knife upward and sideways, piercing the blade through his armpit and directly into his heart. He had no time to react. His heart pumped two more times before he laid dead at my feet. The sound of my blade being removed was sickly satisfying and when it was removed, I used my shirt to wipe it off.

I clicked twice, then spun, meeting the weapon of the attacker. The blade caught my arm, but barely. But my own blade? It jammed into his body at his navel, and I pulled upward, tearing through his skin as he struggled against the pull. His hands wrapped around the hilt of the knife as he tried to pull it out of his body. His fingers touching mine made my skin crawl. Pulling it out was too late now. It wouldn't save him. Still, I yanked hard, removing the knife from his body.

He fell to his knees in front of me, and I knew his eyes would be large as they glazed over. It was part of the process. I could hear the motion of his mouth moving, and blood dripping from his lips, but no words came out, just a gargle of sounds as he fought to form a sentence. Then, he was gone, his body making a slight whoosh sound as it disrupted the flow of air to slump forward.

I smelt Rex near me before I felt his touch. "Take the long way home."

It was a reminder that we lead no one back to our place. We needed to be a hundred percent certain that no one was following and that we were safe. That our people were safe. If they were willing to send a crew of ten people after our single little Doe, what would they send to the underground? What would they do if they knew there was a nest of mutants in one spot, like a target waiting to be hit?

I heard the sirens in the distance as I walked back toward the underground tunnels. I clicked, waiting for the sound to hit me back, seeking the slightly hollow echo of the open drain I came through. When I found it, I slid down before putting back on the drain cover. It wasn't as easy for me. I couldn't simply look both ways and see if anyone was watching. I had to trust that my senses were correct and trust in skills I'd learned to navigate and hope that they didn't let me down.

I took the wrong turns, making sure I heard nothing behind me as I walked. The silence of the night and the tiny squeaks of the underground rats scurrying around for food were the only thing I could hear. My feet dragged through putrid puddles of sludge and water, and my fingers drifted over the icy surfaces of forgotten tiles, bricks, and boards and after an hour of roaming, I allowed myself to find my way back home.

The minute I pulled open the brick wall, I could smell her, and I was sure it was a trick of the mind. How could one smell be engrained so fully in my mind already, after such a short time? I took a moment to stop and inhale, letting my body absorb the comfort of having an omega near us. The scent had changed some, but it was familiar still. Now, though, it mixed with Warren's and was tinged with rex's and mine, and it made my mouth water.

I took the steps slowly, letting the sound of our bustling city underground fill me with comfort as I walked and when I crossed into the cavernous opening, the sounds broke through loudly, echoing. I smiled as I walked, tapping my white cane guide along the surface of the floor. I didn't always need my guide, but in the city where things were constantly changing and children were always under feet, it was a security measure of my own.

No one stopped me as I walked down the man-made walkway. I doubted anyone would. When you come into this place covered with blood, no one asked questions, only accepted that you'd done as you had to do, for the best. And I did. I did what I needed to do to protect my family and to protect Doe. I made my way to the back of the cavern, toward the large carved out room in the side of the boulder wall, the room that I shared with Warren and Rex.

As I grew closer, the scent of them grew stronger, and I knew they were all there. I tapped my cane against a rock, giving a false knock before I pushed open the curtain door and stepped inside. The scent was strong. It sent my desire into overdrive. The claim that Warren had placed on her body was indisputable. He owned her, though I doubt anyone would ever fully own a girl like her.

I heard her gasp before a few footsteps came closer and her skin was against mine. Warren sighed, "I told you, Thea. He is fine."

Thea. The name was like music to my ears, a melody I could never tire of. It rolled through my mind and took up residency there, planting itself as one of the most important things I'd ever heard.

Her hands fumbled over me, searching for injuries. "There's so much blood."

Rex snorted. "I promise you, Doe, none of it is his."

Still, I would not dispute the fact. Her hands on me felt too good to give her a reason to remove them. When she was positive that none of the blood was my own, she pulled away from me for a moment and though I couldn't see, I felt her eyes lay heavy on me as she stared in silence. Finally, she muttered under her breath, "I fucking hate all of you and I don't even know what to do with that information."

Then she took my cheeks in her hands, leaned forward, and kissed me.

CHAPTER
Eleven

WARREN

I watched Thea kiss Ansel, and it had my desire skyrocket. If I thought she was desirable before, it was nothing compared to her pouring herself over one of my men, her men, checking him for injury with genuine concern before kissing him. Still, the selfish part of me wanted her lips on me, her teeth against my skin, her nails clawing into my back as I rode her hard against this stone wall.

Thea.

Her name was as lulling as music, calling to my every cell, begging me to touch her.

And I did. I couldn't help it. My hand fell to her hip as I aligned my body behind hers. This would be an interesting position, of that, I was sure. Sex with her and Ansel would probably become my most favorite of pastimes, but that was probably getting ahead of myself. Fucking her one time didn't mean she'd agree to an encore. I only hoped that after one fuck, she realized there was absolutely no other man out there for her.

I'll admit, there are more alpha males. But none of them as well equipped to protect her and whatever nest we built together. And we would build. We would build a home so strong not a single man or beast could break its defenses. No longer would any of us live in fear, though fear is what we've grown so used to. We would prevail and we would do so strongly so that no one could fight us.

Thea dropped her hands from his cheeks before stepping back from his lips and right into me. She jumped, as if she hadn't realized I was there the whole time. Then she stepped away from me and grabbed Ansel's hand, dragging him over to a basin of water.

She feared me, and she was avoiding it. I disliked the feeling of rejection.

Her fingers grabbed a washcloth, and she dunked it into the warm water before wringing it out. She began gently patting at the blood that smeared over Ansel's skin, treating him as if he was an invalid and he was soaking it up like a plant drank up sunshine. His face beamed over her head as she babied him.

"You are aware he could do that himself." I pointed out.

She glared at me over her shoulder. "I want to make sure he gets it all."

"He'll get it all." Rex added.

"Jealous?" She taunted. I don't know what she expected, but both Rex and I replied yes at the same time.

I reached out and took the cloth from her hand and though she didn't really want to relinquish it, she finally released her grip. "You're bleeding too."

It was the tiniest of trickles honestly, probably not worth a band aid, but it was there. I leaned forward, using my tongue to lick at the blood, and her body tensed under me as her nipples hardened, no doubt remembering what I could do to her body. She cleared her throat. "If I'm bleeding, it's no doubt from being thrown around the apartment."

Rex's face grew angry. "They threw you around?"

I smirked, "No, I did. With my cock pumping inside of her." Her face turned red as she looked down, and I forced her chin up. "There's no need to be shy, little Doe. You think they can't smell my claim on you? You think that when people walk past me, your scent isn't coating my skin. There is no doubt who you belong to."

"I belong to no one." She said it with confidence.

"You belong to us, and the claim you wear on your skin tells everyone just that." I growled.

"I need a shower." She looked me dead in the eye as she made the declaration like that would change things.

"A shower?" I laughed. "A shower will not erase it. The claim is going nowhere. It's already intertwining with your DNA, altering every cell of your make up, Doe. You're mine."

"I didn't agree to that." She looked angry.

"You didn't have to. You were an active participant in riding my cock. The claiming was part of the ride." I smirked.

"I don't want it." She stated again and I'll admit, her defiance when it came to my claim hurt my ego. I reached my hand up to move a strand of hair from her face, and she flinched.

"You're scared of me." I pointed out.

"No."

"You are. You flinched." I felt her heartbeat pick up.

"You killed a man." She muttered.

"So did you. Actually, if we are keeping score, you killed three. I only got one." I shrugged casually.

"I killed a man with daggers. Knives. Constant training and weapons. You killed a man by opening your mouth and, and..."

"Sucking out their soul." I finished. "What of it? I'm far scarier than that, and I've let you know as much from the beginning."

"Your face, it was." She paused as she tried to form words.

"Your face was like staring into a skeleton, Warren. You looked like the very embodiment of death."

"We are mutants, Doe. Mutants. It means we mutate, morph, form into other things and I'm sorry that one of my forms scared you, but I can't change who I am and as scary as it may have been, it saved your life."

"One? One of your forms? What else is there?"

What else? I wish I was confident in telling her the truth. But I doubted she would believe me, anyway. "One day."

She sighed, "Of course. One day. Because I'll be stuck with you for the rest of my life, won't I? Never free."

"You are not a prisoner." Ansel cut in.

"But I'll never be free of you guys either." She observed.

She was right. She wouldn't. But I didn't think she ever would want to be free of us. Not really. Given a little more time, she wouldn't be able to get enough. "We could track you if we desired. Yes. That's true."

"So, what is the plan then? You tell me Warren. Spend the rest of my life just fucking you, hunting with you, having your monsters as I walk around this cave barefoot?"

It would be a fucking lie if I didn't admit that what she spoke didn't sound appealing. I already knew her body was made for me, and I've watched her hunt and kill flawlessly. Watching her walk around a space I created swollen with our child would be the fucking dream. But it was too soon for that. "One day. But that's not what I want for now."

"What do you want for now, Warren?"

"Fucking and assistance." I smirked.

"I don't think you're funny."

"He can't help it." Rex pointed out as he grabbed her hands and squeezed. She instantly relaxed, his calming effect making him the perfect beta. "He's part animal, we all are, and now that he's staked his claim, he won't be able to stay away."

"He didn't, anyway." She deadpanned.

"I mean it. He will want to touch you. Smell you. Fuck you. You're his home now. Your body owns him." Rex licked his lips. "Owns us."

She busied her hands unbuttoning Ansel's bloody shirt and my delta stood taller, his body a hard mass of muscle and tension as her fingers ran over his skin. "What do you need, Warren? Really?"

Smart girl. She knew that there was always a catch and damn it, there was a reason we originally wanted her help. I hadn't planned on her being my omega at the time. I hadn't thought the government even employed a mutant, but she was the in we've been waiting for. I cleared my throat, my mouth suddenly dry, my tongue feeling like sandpaper. "I need to get into the United building. I need to plant an encrypted code into the system and get out. But they have a strong security, and I need your help to get around it."

"They will kill you."

"I doubt it."

"If I help you?" Her chest rose heavily before falling and I couldn't help but bring my finger to her skin, running it down her collarbone.

"If you help me, you're helping us. We are on our way to building a better future, Thea. And in order to do that, we've got to play as dirty as the government."

CHAPTER
Twelve

THEA

I hated him. I hated him with a passion and if I never saw his face again in this lifetime, I'd be the happiest I'd ever been. The other two? They could stay, for now. They hadn't ticked me off nearly as much. But Warren? Who the fuck did he think he was, marking me with his male ego and claiming I was his? I'd never been a single person's belonging in my entire life, and I doubt I would start now.

I refuse to answer if I am willing to help him. I'd let him sweat a bit even though deep down I knew I would. I couldn't help it. I was admiringly drawn to this group like a moth to a flame and fuck if I didn't hate that fact, too. But I would help him. Not because I really wanted to, or because I felt some sort of unity with him that made me want to switch sides, but because they tried to ambush me. My own friends, my coworkers, the very government I worked for, wanted me dead and tried to make it happen and because of that, I needed to know what they were hiding, and I needed to show them they couldn't snuff me out. I'd step outside of the shadows.

I braved a glance over at the men, and they were all getting along like a fucking family. A family I never had. They sat in a circle, playing cards and fuck. Wasn't that the most innocent of things? I saw it, him, in all his terrifying glory, suck a life out of a human and devour it up without even blinking, and now he's sitting there playing Go Fish like he wasn't a killer.

"You can play." He told me for the fourth time when he caught me watching.

"I don't like Go Fish." I smirked.

"We aren't fucking playing Go Fish, and you know it."

Okay. Poker. They were playing Poker. "Looks similar to Go Fish."

I saw Ansel smirk, but it was Rex who sat down his cards and came over. He dropped to his knees in front of me like he had no shame at all in doing so and grabbed my hand. "It bothers you."

"More specific?" He needed to be more specific because right now, every fucking thing bothered me.

"That they came after you." He pondered as he watched. "And that you are here with us."

"Yes."

"Let go of the shadows, Doe. You don't need to hide from us." He kissed my knuckles and instantly the shadows I hadn't realized I was pulling toward me were released, snapping back into place. How did he know? I hadn't even realized I was doing it. I opened my mouth to speak, but he spoke first. "If you think you weren't meant to be here with us, then how do you think we found you, a shadow, in the darkness back at our warehouse?"

I - well, I hadn't really thought about it. I didn't want to. Never had I been spotted in the darkness. I went in, I did the job, I made it out. Never had anyone, man or mutant, spotted me. But they had. They knew I was there, and they had no trouble reaching into the dark and pulling me out of it.

I must have taken too long to answer because Rex continued. "It wasn't by accident, Thea." When they used my name, I swear it did things to my body I did not and would not let myself examine. "Not everyone could see you. Don't be insecure about that. But not everyone around you is an alpha, or a beta, or any part of a hierarchy. Mutants mutated in various ways, and I'll be damned if you believe it was a mistake that you mutated just for us, with a scent that called the very single lone alpha in this city. It wasn't by accident, it wasn't by luck, it was fate, a work of God, whatever you want to believe, that brought you to our warehouse. You were built for us, Thea. Don't believe otherwise. It was the only reason we picked you out of the dark room."

I was torn between wanting to lean down and kiss him and crying because he made me feel so fucking raw and seen and he had no right to do so. I compromised, because I didn't cry, and I wouldn't start with these men. I twisted his fingers into mine and he was right about one thing. Maybe we were meant to be together because his hand sure molded perfectly with my own.

"I don't know who is good and bad anymore." I admitted, and I hated that admission because the men I thought were good, tried to have me killed and the men who I thought were bad, had stood by my side in unity even while a gun was pointed my direction.

"No one has to be good or bad." Rex's tongue came out to wet his lip and its lizard like quality reminded me of just how confused I was on everything. "There just needs to be someone that's willing to be the greater of the two. More good. More civil. More caring."

"And you think you guys are more civil?"

"Fuck no." he laughed, and that sound made the other two men stop what they were doing and look our way. "But I think we care more about the people and our intent is for good. But don't mistake that for us being the good guys. We'll do what it takes to win, Thea. It doesn't matter what that is. We'll slay who needs to be slain, we will climb any obstacle. We aren't good, we aren't bad. We're just really fucking determined to have our way."

This worried me. They would do whatever it takes, that was clear. But how far would they push their boundaries to get what they want? "Including use me."

I shouldn't have said it, but maybe it needed to be said. I needed to know fully where I stood with these men and, well, prepare for the worst and expect the best. Isn't that how the saying goes? I'd like to think they wouldn't harm me, but hell, I hardly knew them and whether it be emotional or physical harm, I need to prepare myself for it now.

I heard the cards drop from the table where Ansel and Warren played, but I didn't look in their direction. I kept my eyes on Rex, expecting him to tell the truth. I couldn't look at anyone else to be truthful. It's all in the eyes and with Ansel's blank stare, I knew nothing would be given away. He truly had a built-in poker face. And Warren? Every time I glanced his direction, my heart did weird things and I couldn't trust myself not to believe everything he said. He made my body do weird unfamiliar things and my mind was a cloud of confusion when he was near. But Rex, Rex was safe.

I felt the shadow of Warren loom over me as he stopped next to Rex, but I refused to look up. "You think we would hurt you to get what we want?"

Don't look up, don't look up. I kept my gaze on Rex. Counting the scales along his neck was oddly soothing and I refused to look away from it. "I think I don't know you well enough to know otherwise."

"Look at me." He demanded and well, I didn't. I felt his energy pulsing through the air, and I didn't want to look at him, afraid of what I'd see when I did. "I said, look at me."

Like a pull I couldn't ignore, my head snapped up and our eyes met. "Yes?"

"We will do whatever it takes to get what we want. Rex did not lie about that. Whatever it fucking takes, whoever we have to fucking kill. Don't be delusional enough to think that we aren't killers, murderers, thieves. We are. We are the monsters that lurk under beds and hide in dark alleys, we are the monsters that fear is made of. But we are only monsters to the outside world. Inside these walls, when it's just the four of us, we are a slave to you. We'd gladly lay in the shadows to be close to you. We'd give up anything, and I mean anything, in order to protect you. You are ours. And we'd destroy everything in this world, ignite it in flame. But you? We'd never hurt you."

I wanted to discount his words as nonsense because they just met me. They knew nothing about me. Hell, they just learned my real name, and that wasn't even my choice. But I couldn't deny that what they said, coming from Warren's lips, felt true. My heart was telling me so and though I tried to ignore it, I couldn't. Maybe there really was some sort of deeper connection here, something I couldn't quite place yet, but should believe exists.

"Okay." I got the words out, even as my throat scratched, and my eyes burned. Shit, why did I feel this way? I'd not cried in so damn long and suddenly, being around these men, that's all I wanted to do. They weakened me. That had to be it. I was an assassin, but around them, I was moments away from becoming a blubbering baby.

"Okay." Warren nodded as his eyes burned into mine.

"Okay." I said again because, fuck, I was an idiot.

"Okay." Rex smirked before standing up, stretching to his

full height then reaching down and tossing me over his shoulder in a blink. "Time for bed."

I squirmed against him, trying to get free, but Rex's grip was tight against me. "I can walk perfectly fucking fine."

His head turned toward me, and he bit my hip, sending a bite of pain through me. Pain that swiftly had my core heating and me squirming. He inhaled deeply, a rumble vibrating through his chest. "You can, but I'd rather you didn't. I like you where you are."

"Y'all are a bunch of fucking cavemen." I growled the words.

"We are. But when was the last time someone took care of you?" My body pitched forward as my feet landed on the mattress set up on the floor. His hands released me, and he stared me down, daring me to argue more. "You don't need to be so damn independent when you've got us at your beck and call. Get to sleep, we'll be here shortly."

Them? As in all of us sleeping on here? I looked around, noticing that it was a wide space of multiple mattresses pressed together. I just never thought I could sleep with all of them, or maybe I never realized that we all would sleep together. "Are we…"

"Are we all sharing this? Yes. Are you over thinking? Also, yes." Rex smirked and damn it, every time he did that a slight dimple appeared, and it made my feet a bit swoony. Fuck, I didn't swoon. I murdered. I murdered at the United Government's whim for so fucking long that I'd been brainwashed into not even realizing that's what I was doing. But swoon? I never did that.

"Okay." Fuck, why can't I think of more articulate things to say around these men? All I've got is okay, like I'm an agreeable puppy for them to pass around and do as they please.

"Okay." He said with a laugh and damn it, all the attention on me made me uncomfortable. I could feel Warren's eyes burning into me. And Ansel? He may not see, but I could feel his energy pushing against mine as he felt out the area.

I watched as they turned away, leaving me in the bed area. I looked around, allowing myself to see for the first time the space I'd be living in. And... fuck, why were men so messy and careless? I crawled over to the mounds of pillows and blankets and began grabbing each pillow and placing them around the bed. It was a huge spot, taking up the size of three queen beds. Even with the three of them and just me, I couldn't imagine using all of that space. Unless... I bet Rex was a crazy sleeper. He seemed like he would be. Warren, I bet he picked a single calculated spot and stuck with it. And Ansel, well, would he go to the same place to sleep each time, out of familiarity since he couldn't see change?

Oh god.

Should I be changing things?

Was I making myself too much at home?

I looked around, my eyes taking in all the things I moved and adjusted as I was deep in my thought.

Pillows lined the bed by both the head and the side, creating a cushiony barrier and blankets laid flat along each of the mattresses, then folded by the head of the bed because I liked the feel of blankets snuggled against my face as I drifted off to sleep. Blankets meant comfort and I couldn't get enough. I wished I had thought about grabbing my favorite blanket before leaving my apartment. I wonder if they'd let me go back.

Fuck. I needed to go back. I had my things. My notebooks. My files.

I turned, ready to announce that I needed to make the trip back to my place, only I hadn't expected all the men to be staring back at me.

"What?" the word came out way more aggressive than I intended.

"You're nesting." Warren muttered before swallowing hard, making his Adam's apple bob. "It's making me hard."

"I could sneeze, and you'd get hard." I rolled my eyes. "I don't even know what nesting is."

In front of me, Rex dropped to his knees. "Can I come on the bed?"

His question was odd but also, I appreciated it. I'd worked hard on this damn bed, making it comfortable and lord knows I would rather die than make a bed in real life. Fitted sheets and I are not on friendly terms. "Just don't fuck up the blankets."

A smirk that gifted me with another dimple. "I wouldn't dream of it, Doe."

He crawled carefully toward me while the other two men stood by. When Rex reached me, his arm went around my waist and he pulled me, causing me to stumble downward, laying me on the blankets. His chest rumbled, the feeling so damn comforting. He was the comforting one, the one who made me feel welcomed and safe, even if I knew danger was near. And it was near. It was standing feet away watching me like I grew two heads, two heads he wanted to devour with his sharp teeth.

And fuck, his teeth were sharp.

I saw every single one of them as his face turned to bone and his body morphed into something so completely unrecognizable. The thought and reminder both terrified and allured me. What was it about this man that was so damn addicting, even when I knew I should repel away at all costs?

Rex inhaled the scent of my hair and I thought about fighting it and pulling away, but I was tired, and this was nice, even if it was a temporary solution to a larger problem. The problem being that my employer wants me dead. My employer wants me dead, and I doubt they would stop at anything to get it done. Why? I wasn't sure. But I couldn't help but wonder if what Warren suspected had a grain of truth. Could I really be the key the mutants had been looking for to growing their population? There had to be more out there. I doubt they were being hunted.

A sharp exhale brought my thoughts back to Rex as he spoke. "Nesting means making it your home. Building a nest of comfort, so if you went into heat, you would be as comfortable as possible."

I snorted. "Go into heat. That's not going to fucking happen."

I felt my skin burn. How bold of them to think they could talk about my body and its function. It was Warren who spoke next. "We're going off assumptions here, Doe. No one really knows how it works. We'd never met another group with a hierarchy that had found an omega before. But that right there was definitely a nesting habit. You were so long in thought you didn't even realize we were watching."

"Or listening." Ansel added.

Rex's hand flattened against my stomach before slowly sliding downward and I fought to stay still. "You're reading too much into it. I was moving things into a logical order."

"Our logical order was the way you found it." Warren's voice was thick. "Can I step on the bed?"

Why the fuck are they asking me? It literally is their bed. I'm just borrowing it. "It's yours."

"No. It's ours." He stated before he toed off his shoes and then bent at his knees until they hit the surface of the mattress.

He crawled toward me, stopping when his eyes were level with my own, and let his body melt down into the pile of blankets. I held my breath, thinking he would say something, make some sort of vile comment or suggestion, maybe something that I would deem ridiculous and dismiss, but he didn't. After what felt like a lifetime, the urge to blink burned the back of my eyes, but I refused to be the one to break our stare. I was strong. I knew I was. I didn't want him to know that deep down, I was feeling weaker than I had since I was a child, lost and alone.

He blinked first, before letting his body fall the rest of the way to the mattress, his nose instantly going to my neck as he snuggled himself in deep. His hand found my waist, not caring that Rex's arm was already around me. "Go to sleep, my little Doe. You've had a busy day."

Then his chest rose and fell as he drifted off to sleep.

CHAPTER
Thirteen

WARREN

I never fell asleep so fast in my life and it wasn't something I thought possible. I just wanted to comfort her for a single moment, lay close to her and absorb her scent into my every pore as she drifted off to sleep. But then when I laid next to her, my nose snug against her skin, I was out. I closed my eyes for a single second and next thing I know I was blinking awake hours later to the sight of Thea next to me, sandwiched between my body, Rex, and Ansel's.

My chest puffed out with pride as I watched them. My cock stirred and though I knew I shouldn't, I let my finger run along the curves of her skin, tracing each dip as I moved. A moan slipped past her lips and her scent blossomed through the air. I knew she was asleep, but even asleep, she couldn't fight wanting us. She still had on that tiny fucking pencil skirt and every time I looked at it, all I could think about is how well it looked bunched around her waist as I pounded my cock into her.

My finger traveled back down her body and before I knew

it, two of them were teasing against the skin of her inner thighs, walking a trail upward and she didn't fight it. Her body leaned into my touch and her legs relaxed. I shouldn't, I knew, but when I looked up and Rex's knowing eyes burned into me, I couldn't resist. Fuck, I didn't want to.

Rex's hands grabbed at the material close to her knees and yanked up, pulling the material out of the way, and gifting me the view of her luscious, bare skin. Fuck, I didn't deserve her... Men like Rex and I, we barely deserved attention from females, a repentance for the crimes we had committed. But here she was, in her sleep, gifting us the honor of touching her.

Another moan escaped her as she leaned back into Rex. Her head lolled against his shoulder as he used his thigh to part her legs. Shamelessly, her body rubbed up against his thigh, seeking the deliverance of pleasure. She'd be angry, I knew. But fuck, when she was angry, she was so fucking beautiful that I'd made it my goal to cause her fury every fucking day for the rest of my life, anyway.

Not waiting for my demands, Rex pushed his hands into her panties, cupping her sex before sliding his hand upward just enough to rub his fingers over her clit. She whimpered. The sound was like a cry of approval, a beg for us to continue even if she wasn't fully lucid. She would be, this I was positive. And when she was, I hoped her eyes rimmed with the fire my beast craved to see and her actions reflected the fury that fueled my lust.

I danced my finger around the seam of her panties, teasing her with promises. Her chest was already rising and falling, Rex already fanning her flame of desire with his fingers slowly circling her clit. But when she came, I wanted it to be me she directed her anger at, my face she cursed as she rode her high of lust to the other side of sanity.

I slipped my finger into the barrier of cloth, pushing it to the side to expose her bare skin to me and the sight of her, the sight of her bare pussy on display, in the faint light of a candle burning, made the beast inside of me roar its ownership. Never in my life had I been so thankful for superior night vision. Never in my life had I wanted to use it more, zoom in on every detail and commit them to memory to play repeatedly every waking hour. Never until now. When my fingers glided over the smooth skin, her whimpers of want broke into cries of need.

She was wet, weeping for me, begging for me to feel her and fuck. It was tempting. The way her body clamped down on my cock yesterday brought me to bliss I didn't even know was possible. I never wanted to leave her body, evident by how much resistance my knot put up when it came time to remove my cock. It didn't help that watching her murder a fucker while I was seated balls deep was like the greatest aphrodisiac known to man. It was a fucking sight. The exact moment I knew this girl was mine. No others. Mine. And I'd prove to her just that, even if I spent the rest of my forsaken life doing so.

My fingers dipped between her lips, coating my fingers in moisture and want before removing it. Fuck, she was soaking for us, and she was still not fully lucid, still walking the line between sleep and wake, dancing between the pull of both. I brought my finger up, offering it up to Rex, who leaned forward greedily, sucking my fingers in his mouth as he cleared her essence off of them. He closed his eyes, bliss taking over his face as his system recognized what I already knew. She was ours. Ours to keep. Ours to cherish. Ours to own.

I pulled my fingers away and for a moment, his tongue chased them, not wanting to lose the taste of her from his lips. But I couldn't wait much longer, I needed to feel her body tighten around my fingers, needed to feel her body weep from its want of my touch and if I didn't see her face as she shattered into euphoria, I might die before the day was out.

My finger entered her body effortlessly, her body already welcoming me as it flexed and squeezed. I closed my eyes for a moment, letting my mind and body absorb the feel of her, craving so much more but not willing to take it, at least not yet. Not until she understood, not until she realized she would forever be ours. Then I'd take her every fucking way, sleeping or not, because she would know that it wasn't malice that drove me, but the undeniable need for her nearness, to please her, to own her.

I pulled my finger out, sliding two back in and fuck, she was so fucking petite next to us. Her body was so damn tiny I swear getting just two inside of her was a tight fit. It made me wonder how her body took my full cock and my knot without a single cry of pain. I worked my fingers in her body slowly, pushing in and pulling out, stretching her enough to fit a third and even in slumber, she was going wild. Her body riding my fingers and rubbing against Rex's thigh, her chest heaving, her face so fucking pink as her body heated.

She was getting close, I could feel it, I could tell by the way her -

A tiny hand was around my throat, her fingers squeezed and when I brought my eyes to her face, the electrical blue orbs stared at me. "Don't fucking stop, finish it."

Her demand nearly had me coming in place. I listened, her fingers not loosening on my throat. If I was human, I was sure I'd have already lost consciousness, but my body had long ago left humanity behind and in its place, a man who strived for the brutality and ate up the fear of the common human. Her thumb pressed into my pulse as I worked my fingers into her, her body leaned into Rex and together we were a unity of the taboo. Three outcasts, three lovers. Three was a beautiful fucking number. Not as beautiful as four. Four of us against this fucking world and I knew that with this girl on our side, we'd win it all.

I could hear her heartbeat faster, feel her pulse increase,

and with her eyes that burned into me so fucking raw, I knew she had little time before her body exploded around my digits and she lost all control. I twisted my wrist, angling my fingers just right, then I curved them, using the tips to press into her body and rub against the nerves that begged for attention. Her eyes watered up as her mouth opened in a silent scream and then without warning, she exploded.

Her body squeezed and tightened around my fingers, pulling me deeper as her hand around my throat tightened, cutting off all my air. The silent scream broke into a gasp as she sucked in oxygen. Her body squirmed against Rex's as she tried to pull away, but fuck her, I didn't care if the assault on her body was too much. I was chasing it until the end, forcing her to come as hard as she fucking could, not caring if she was damn near begging for a reprieve.

I wouldn't grant it.

There would be no reprieve until she rode her bliss to the very end. Even as my vision began to spot in the corners as her fingers dug in so fucking tight, I prayed she would leave her marks of ownership against my sensitive skin. Her chest rose and her fingers released and without even realizing it was happening, I gasped, taking in the air my lungs craved.

Then I crashed my lips to hers, devouring every single noise she offered as her orgasm ebbed and my chest burned with the need for more air. I didn't grant myself the pleasure of it. I didn't need it. I'd rather die of strangulation and suffocation, with my lungs burning so intensely I'd think they were on fire, then part myself from her lips at this very moment.

The movement of her lips slowed. The frantic energy that surged around us less intense, and when her body stopped pulsing around my fingers, I dared her to finally move. Against the revolt of every single cell in my body, I pulled my fingers free of her as Rex slowed his assault on her clit. Both our chests rose and fell rapidly, our eyes locked and hers burned so damn intently. I swore the aqua moved and swirled with emotions I'd never recognize.

When she could finally speak, her words came out as a harsh whisper. "I fucking hate you."

I brought my fingers to my mouth, without losing eye contact, and licked them like I was tasting a fucking popsicle. "It tastes like love to me." She growled her disapproval and when she opened her mouth to speak, I stuck my fingers in her mouth, letting her taste just how much she wanted us. Letting her essence tell the story of what our bodies do to her and how easily we can get her off. "Close your mouth."

I made the order putting all my strength behind it and though her eyes burned with anger, her mouth closed around my fingers, and I didn't have to issue a single fucking order as her tongue swirled around them, tasting them before she sucked against the skin. Fuck me, I was weak. The single act was so damn hot I was about to come without a single finger of hers touching my cock.

I pulled my fingers free, closing my eyes against the alluring sound they made as they popped free of her lips. Rex leaned in, his voice a whisper as he nuzzled against her neck. "You taste as good as you smell, Little Doe, and I can't wait to devour you myself."

She turned her head, her eyes locking with Rex's and without a second warning she captured his lips, kissing him, consuming him, searing the truth for me. This girl, she was ours. There was no fucking doubt about it and if she tried to run, I'd find her. I'd track her. I'd kill anything in my path in order to keep her.

CHAPTER
Fourteen

REX

I could still smell her in the air, the faint musk of her essence taunting and teasing us from this morning's activities. She could tease all she wants and declare her hatred, but her body wanted Warren something fierce. The moment he was touching her, her body went wild, craving him and fuck. I was a selfish bastard because I was willing to piggyback on the ride just to feel the combustion.

I clicked the switch before turning it, setting the flame on our tiny camp stove we allowed ourselves inside our quarters. Was it the safest? Absolutely not. But did it allow me to make my girl pancakes after a morning of bliss? It sure the fuck did. Who cared about safety when she was fed and happy? And I thought we'd make her happy. We just needed some time to show her, some time for her to adjust to the life we led. The less savory of lives.

"Think she will stay?" Ansel whispered, and I looked up, not even hearing him approach.

"I fucking hope so." I growled the words, a bit of possessiveness rumbling inside of me. "We need to tell her the plan."

"It's too fucking soon for it." Ansel commented as he looked down at the stove. I knew he couldn't see what I was doing, but he could hear the slight rumble of the flames as they burned. "Pancakes?"

"And eggs." I added.

"Want me to cut up some fruit?"

"Have at it." I didn't have to tell him where he could find the supplies or the produce. Navigating our space was like second nature to him and he knew what he was doing and even if he had no vision, he handled a knife easily, doing so like a pro.

I had a stack of pancakes already made and a few sunny-side-up eggs lining a plate when Warren and Thea walked into our area. She didn't seem angry, which was a good sign. But she didn't look like she was ready to fall to Warren's feet and worship him, either. "Enjoy the shower?"

Warren smirked, and Thea shrugged. I suspected there was more than just showering going on in our private facility. "It was a nice setup, I'll admit."

A set up of community and private showers was one luxury we allowed ourselves down here. But our private shower, the one built for the three... well, now four of us, was top-notch. Who would have thought that past us would have planned for future us? We never actually thought that theory was true. We never imagined finding an omega among the sea of humans and now? Well, Warren claimed her without her even realizing it, and there was no fucking escaping us. The moment he locked himself inside her body, there was no fucking going back. She was it for us.

I tried not to think of our ownership, of my desire to feel her skin against mine and taste her want on my lips. It wasn't the time for it, though I sure as fuck could make it the time. I closed my eyes for a moment, pushing the desire down. "If you're hungry, there are pancakes, eggs and fruit."

I knew she was hungry. She had to be. She hardly ate last night before she crashed out on the adorable and comfy little nest she created and, after the activities of the early hours, she needed some substance. Warren placed a hand on her back, guiding her forward when she didn't move to get food. Without saying a word, he piled high a plate of fluffy pancakes, eggs, and fruit. Then he placed it in front of her and forced her to sit.

Warren, the alpha, opted to serve.

If I had a notebook nearby, I'd write this down in history as a momentous occasion. Sure, he was all about the community and helping, but to serve someone, from his hands to theirs, offer a plate of food when they clearly could get it themselves, well, that was an act unheard of. She took the offering though, and didn't argue when we all knew she wanted to do nothing more than tell him no out of spite.

After lifting a fork full of pancake to her lips, she muttered, "I need to go back to my apartment."

She said the words so lightly that I wasn't sure if she wanted us to hear them. Still, all our heads turned toward her, and the words fell from our mouths in unison. "No."

She dropped the fork onto her plate. "I don't think you've got a say in this. I need things."

"We'll buy you things."

"Some things can't just be bought." She huffed.

"Like what?" Warren ladled his plate with food, trying not to let his anger show and he did well at it, if you didn't see his fingers squeezing the plate so hard it threatened the ceramic to shatter in his grasp.

She licked her lips nervously. "My blanket, for one."

"Thea." Warren groaned. "You have blankets here."

"It's not the same. You can't simply deny a girl the luxury of her favorite blanket."

"I'm denying you the luxury of your favorite blanket."

Her fork that she had just picked up, dropped to the plate again. "Warren, you do not own me."

"I don't." He admitted. "Monetarily. But physically you're mine, and though I know full well you will spend every waking second defying me; on this I'd wish you wouldn't. They will watch the place, waiting for your return."

"You're paranoid." Thea hissed.

"I'm experienced." He pointed out.

"I'll pull the shadows." She offered. But pulling the shadows wasn't the solution to everything.

"You think shadows will hide objects moving? Be smart. You're not going back there and that's final. Now, on to our plan. We've been watching the building that the United Government operates out of. You've been there?"

She blinked a few times, her eyes looking like they were trying to come to some resolve. After her decision was made, her chest rose and puffed out before she replied. "Yes."

"Think you can draw a map of the inside?"

She bit her lip. There was a war inside her of good and evil, and she wasn't sure where she stood or which side would be the victor. I spoke up, trying to persuade her. "They were your home, Thea. I get that it's hard to just give up information on them when they were a part of you for so long, using you. But they tried to kill you. We all saw it."

"Not me." Ansel smirked.

I glared at him, though he was oblivious to it. "They tried to kill you and you know this to be true. Why would you protect them when they failed to protect you like you had trusted them to do so?"

Her back straightened, a sign of a girl who spent her entire existence fighting for herself, with no one at her side to help her. "I can protect myself. Warren saw it. Clearly he knows it's true."

"You can." He nodded. "But-"

I cut Warren off because we all knew he was going to be so fucking caveman like and scare her away. We need progress, not regression. "But you don't have to always protect yourself, not with us around. We want to protect you." I drew out the words to get them across to her. "In fact, we get off on doing so."

"I don't want to get you off." She muttered, with no emotion behind it.

"Sounded like someone was getting off this morning." Ansel added, and I swear to God I was about ready to throw a fucking pancake at his face.

"Ansel, you're not fucking helping." Warren turned toward her. "I'll admit, helping you, my sweet little damsel, makes me hard as a fucking rock, and I crave that feeling of the rescue. But what he means is sometimes it's easier to take on responsibility and weight when others will carry some of the load. They did not protect you, but we will."

Of course, she hardly knew us. I was aware of that and so was Warren, but we had given no indication of dishonesty. We would protect her. We would cherish her. We would be the family she lacked for so damn long. But trust was hard earned with people like us, and it was something that went both ways. We trusted her. Knowing what she was and what she was sent here to do, we trusted her. We let her go back home and maybe she hadn't ousted us to the agency, but fuck if she didn't bring questions with them to light. The target on us had widened. Our time running out. Act now or lose the chance.

"We need your help." I admitted. "We need this information."

"Why?"

"It's not just the local government, it's wide. Up to the very sitting president." My eyes met Warren's for a moment, feeling his anger at the very mention. "They are targeting specific mutants and we need to know why."

"They pose a threat. Isn't that obvious?" She leaned back in her chair. "We all do."

"They didn't find you threatening until you paired up with us." I pointed out.

"Because by associating with criminals, I became one."

"You think that's it?" It wasn't. "If so, you've already been marked with their scarlet letter. Might as well help us out because there is no point of return from here."

It was true. If they were after her based solely on her friendliness with us, she was already an outcast. Though we all knew differently. She was a threat. A fucking adorable and beautiful, sexy and sensual threat. But a threat all the same. They used her ability until she no longer served the purpose they intended, until she was no longer blinded to their deceit and now? Well, now it was our turn to wrap ourselves in her shadows and bring truths to light.

"We need a map of the inside." I continued. "We need to know where the computer mainframe is."

"What do you plan to do?" She looked suspicious.

"Get in, insert a drive into it, download our programs, and get out."

"What type of programs?" Jesus, they used her to assassinate? She could have been better used to interrogate.

"We're working with another sector."

Thea cut Warren off. "There is more?"

"More people wanting freedom. Endlessly. More than you can imagine. All hiding, hoping. Praying for the day they can walk the streets safely." He paused, looking for a visual reaction, before clearing his throat. "We are working with others to view their systems. This is just the first step. We need to figure out the motives and what they are doing before we can possibly form a proper plan."

"But the plan you want to form, where does it go?"

There was a long pause, and it was now or never. He could trust her, or he couldn't. The extent of information was up to him. Neither Ansel nor I were willing to broach it. "Presidency."

There was a sharp intake of air, and her face reflected the horror I knew she would display. She'd been conditioned to believe the government was for the good, but her conditioning never taught her the bad they tried so fucking hard to hide. It was a constant game of manipulation and the people? The people were the victims, playing the obedient marionette, moving in whatever direction the strings were pulled.

"That's impossible. You are one person, Warren. One." She shook her head. "You think you can be president?"

"I don't want to be."

"Then who?"

"It's not important. It's a simple task to walk into the White House. But to get control needs preparation."

"A simple task." She snorted. "Yeah, if you know the president." There was silence that followed because she didn't realize just how close she hit to the truth. "You don't, do you? Know the president?"

"Will you help us? Or not?" Warren prompted.

"You want me to go in, plant the program and get out? That's it?"

She was so used to thinking singular, but she hadn't realized she didn't have to. Warren was the one who answered first. "No. I want us. We go in, we do what we need to, and we get out. I want you in the shadows the whole time. I will not risk your safety."

"But you would risk your own." She pointed out.

"It's not a risk, as you saw." Her whole body shivered as she no doubt remembered what Warren was capable of. "I don't take joy in the consumption, just so you know. At least, not when they aren't actively threatening me or those I deem mine. Would I like to go into that office and have everything go smoothly? Yes. But, if need be, I know where my powers lie and how to use them."

Powers. Because wasn't that a fucking joke? The government unwillingly handed us the gift of power and abilities. The gift of superiority. They view the superiority as a weakness because it makes us a unique form of strength against them.

"Will you help?" I locked eyes with her, and I dared myself to not look away. I willed myself to not blink. I urged myself to hold strong, even when the intensity of her eyes burned into me so damn hard that I felt utterly raw and exposed.

Then she blinked. The stare we held, broken, as she bit her lip and looked between the three of us. "I'll help. But I'm tired of hiding in the shadows."

CHAPTER
Fifteen

ANSEL

She was in. The moment she agreed to the plan, I felt tension release from Warren with a snap. We needed her and though I knew he didn't agree to her not using her shadows to his advantage, I knew he sought comfort because we were there. Together, we'd protect her. I had no doubt about that. There wasn't a single one of us who wasn't willing to go to the ends of this world to protect what we claimed.

And there is no mistaking that fact. She'd been claimed.

Just standing close to her has her radiating the scent of Warren, leaving no doubt who placed his claim. Repeatedly, if my heightened senses weren't wrong. It was all part of the process. I knew what was Warren's, was all of ours. And the more he imprinted himself on her and inside of her, the greater chance it would detour enemies who had an interest in her, at least of the mutant variety. It was an infatuation, an obsession, an urge he couldn't fight, and truthfully, I doubted he wanted to.

"There are alarms on every door, then?" He questioned her as she drew out a map for him.

She was sitting on his lap, his choice not hers. She tried to get away for all of five seconds before she gave in once he claimed limited space. It was a lie. We were all capable of standing, but he just wanted her nearby. He had to have it. "They are. And guarded by at least one guard. However, the windows, particularly the ones in the attic, have nothing protecting them as a point of entrance."

He took his nose out of her hair where it was buried, his brows furrowed. "That's a large oversight."

"It is." She nodded her agreement.

"How did you stumble upon this information?"

Rex sat a plate of cookies and a cup of coffee in front of the girl. I could tell by the scraping of the ceramic against the wood and the scent that wafted toward me. He couldn't help himself. He was a nurturer at heart. "My first time in the building, I pulled the shadows and explored. I never lock myself into a place without knowing points of escape and entrances."

It was a habit born to those who lived a life alone and in constant fear. A protection tactic. "You are here without knowing these things."

She inhaled, looking as if she carried the weight of the world. "Against my better judgement, clearly. I'm trusting you three."

Trust, it was such a heavy and fragile thing. One tiny little ding to its exterior could cause the whole thing to crumble to the ground. I refused to let that happen. She gifted us with this trust and I'd protect it at all costs.

I clicked my tongue, listening for the tiny vibrational changes as the sound bounced off the surrounding objects, then I leaned forward, grabbing a cookie off the plate. Holding it up triumphantly, I stated, "Trust comes with cookies."

"Cookies you didn't bake." Rex added.

"Would you want me to bake? I will." I started to stand because I'm always about proving a point, but Thea's hand gripped my arm, halting me.

A shiver instantly went through my body, and I froze. Her touch was like ice against my warm skin and the contrast was a bliss I didn't know existed. Was this what came with Warren claiming her? This new effect on me? I swallowed hard, waiting for her to speak, wishing for the first time that I could see the face I was missing out on. The face that had our leader so damn infatuated he would throw away all his carefully planned notions, disregarding all caution, just to have her on our side.

"We don't need you to cook, Ansel. You'll get hurt."

Would I get hurt? Possibly though it wasn't likely. She didn't know me well enough yet to understand that my senses were astronomical. But would what I cooked taste good? Absolutely not. I could not see what I was measuring or figure out what measuring cup was what, or hell, even to read a fucking recipe.

At her concern, both Rex and Warren snorted, and she questioned them. "What?"

"What?" Warren bellowed in amusement. "I assure you that Ansel doesn't need vision to be the most capable man here. God took his sight because he knew if he had that too, he would be unstoppable."

"I don't think it works that way." She sighed before turning her attention to me. "They think highly of you for sure."

Bless her for not realizing what I was fully capable of. "I've earned it."

I used this moment of concern to my advantage. I snagged her hand and pulled, allowing her to stumble into my lap. The switch in her location caused a rumble from Warren. "Hey that was mine."

"Was." I smirked as I wrapped my arms around her waist.

She really felt perfect here, like she was meant for my lap and to be wrapped in my arms. "Now she's mine."

"I'm not an object." She protested.

I felt Rex against my leg as he sat on the floor, wanting to be close to her. His head moved against my thighs as he nuzzled into her and, without a thought, her hand fell to his head. It was his superpower. The ability to calm and add comfort, soothe. He did it so flawlessly that even this trained killer in my hands hadn't realized she was stroking his hair. He loved it, though. Fingers in Rex's hair were his own equivalent to heaven, and when we were younger, rejected teens living in the underground world, it used to be the only way Warren and I could get him to drift off to sleep.

I buried my nose against her back, inhaling deep as I took in the scents of her skin and the essence of Warren. Perfection. I felt my cock stir, already reaching for her, but she said nothing as she continued to lean forward and make notes on the map. When the scraping of the pencil against the paper stopped and her body leaned back into me, I said. "I can't see what she's written." Another snort from Warren. "But my guess is the best bet is to send Doe and Warren through the window. It's imperative that they get in, get the drive inserted, download the file, and get out. Undetected. Rex and I, we'll go in the front door if we have to or slip in elsewhere and wait to cause a scene. It's a classic distract from the real threat scenario, but when it comes to mutants, they don't deem us as smart enough to carry through with such planning."

"Absolutely not." She stated before anyone else got a word in. "You'll get hurt."

"She is cute, isn't she?" I asked Warren and Rex. "Thea, this isn't about me. The fight we're after is greater than me. If I get hurt, I get hurt. But I won't. I think you underestimate my capabilities. I don't have vision. That's true. But not having vision only handicaps my ability to see the face that has captured both Rex's and Warren's obsessions. Not seeing my enemy strengthens me. I can't feel guilt for eyes for which I don't see the life fading. Humans depend heavily on what they can see and don't trust the things they cannot. They don't understand that something as simple as a heartbeat can give away a hiding spot, or that someone's scent can tell you if they are ready to strike based purely on the adrenaline that seeps out of their pores. They think they have an advantage because of sight, but sight is their disadvantage."

"He's right." Warren reassured her.

"I just-"

Without warning, Warren picked up an apple from the table, throwing the fruit directly at my head. I didn't see him pick it up, obviously. But the sound the apple made as it cut through the air alerted me to its destination. My hand shot up, catching the fruit before it smashed into my nose. Without a second thought, I brought the apple to my mouth and took a bite.

Point proven.

"Ansel and Rex up front, Warren and I through the window." She continued as if that hadn't just happened. "And to get up to the window?"

"Climb or fly?" Warren suggested.

"Is that even..."

"Yes." I replied. "I can fly you up."

Her body jolted in my grip. Her hands instantly wrapping around me as they started running rapidly over my back. She even climbed up on her knees and shifted my shirt so she could peer down inside of it. The action and curiosity of it made me smile. "How?"

"We're mutants. We morph and mutate Doe. Just like you wrap shadows and become unseen. They don't use the saying blind as a bat for nothing. My mutation took that saying and ran with it."

"I- I guess I just assumed..."

"That you would see me toting around large wings if it was true? No. That isn't how having the ability to mutate works. You've spent a lot of time brushing shoulders with the humans. There is still so much you haven't learned about your kind."

She settled herself back down on my lap. "We fly up there, enter through the window, then sneak down to the main-frame computer and pray no one sees us?"

Warren's throat cleared. "No. You'll pull your shadow around us both."

"I can't."

"You can."

Warren was so fucking confident in this, and he was going on a theory he had. But she didn't have to know that. She didn't have to know that when you linked yourself together, there was a slight chance you took on the ability to protect each other and adapt your mutations as such. His other theory? Over time, you take on traits. Now, as cool as that would be, I wondered if he was wrong on that front. I'd been with Warren and Rex my whole life it seems, and not once had we taken on each other's traits. But neither of us were an Omega like her. Neither of us could tie us all together like this girl in my lap.

She seemed skeptical but unwilling to argue further. "We'll see then."

"We will."

Literally, the tension and stubbornness between these two was so thick in the air every second they were near each other that everyone might suffocate on it. "How much do you know about technology?"

"None." Rex answered for her. "She didn't even own a television."

"It's a waste of space." Thea tried to defend herself.

"You had plenty of space." Rex made a rumble sound as he nuzzled against her thigh.

"I'm going off the assumption you know nothing. We'll get our tech guy on the line and work out a plan and give you a quick lesson," I stated.

"We can send Warren in. I'll stand guard."

"Logically, that would make sense." I mused. "However, as this is a new pairing, Warren needs to protect you, not the other way around. There is no way anyone could pair with him in this but you. And his need to protect you and you alone means he has to stand guard."

"I literally can hide in the shadow where no one can see me." She sputtered out her logic, and I got it. I knew where she was coming from. However, whatever alpha DNA is in his blood doesn't care.

"I made a promise to protect you." He growled.

And there it was. "I could protect you more."

Oh, that was a hit.

"I don't need protecting. You've only seen a little of what I can do." He stated.

"Don't be flashing fire looking eyes at me." His eyes flashed fire? Hum. I'm not shocked. I just wished I could see it. "Your big oaf of a body will give you away in seconds."

"Then wrap your shadows around me." He demanded.

"I can't."

"You fucking can." At least he hoped.

Rex, the peacekeeper of the bunch, always cut in. "Thea, it needs to be you going in there because Warren is too broad and his arms too thick to fit behind the machines. He needs to protect, and he will protect at all costs, but his size makes it impossible for him to get the job done."

She hummed under her breath before muttering. "Yeah, I know all about his size." She shifted in my lap, and she wasn't fooling any of us. Even if we heard not a single word, her scent would have been a giveaway of what she was thinking. "If I can't pull my shadows around him?"

"You will."

"You're so fucking confident, Warren. What happens when things don't go your way? Will you eat my soul too?" It's like this little wisp of a female enjoyed poking the dragon.

"Honey, I've already eaten your soul and if I remember correctly, you begged for more."

I felt her whole-body heat in my lap and judging by the scent she was giving off, it was equal parts arousal and mortification. "I never beg."

"Our realities must vary then." Oh, he was smug as fuck right now, I can tell you that. I'd known Warren long enough to have that tone memorized. "If you cannot shield me, the plan stays the same. Only your swiftness inside the room might be more dire."

"I already hate it here." She grumbled, and I knew she was just pouting, but damn it, I wanted to show her all the reasons she would love it.

"Because I might be in danger?" Why must he taunt her by searching for compliments?

"No." I heard the bitterness dripping from her voice. "Because I'm forced to be in proximity to you."

I cleared my throat loudly. It was clear if these two were going to coexist, they would need a constant mediator. "So then, the plan is set."

"Generally." Warren muttered.

"The details of the inside are small in comparison. We'll have men observing for a few days. We'll hit Monday?" I asked Warren.

"That's perfect. I'll set up our crew." Warren's clothes rustled as he stood.

"Wait." Thea jerked in my arms. "Why Monday? Crew? Like more of you?"

Poor girl didn't even know how much more there was. Thousands of us, waiting to rise.

"Nothing, and I mean nothing, happens on a Monday." I felt Rex's vibrations through Thea as he spoke against her leg.

"No one will expect a Monday Infiltration. And crew? The world doesn't revolve around just us. There's so many more who want freedoms they were never granted."

She made a sound in her throat as if she was fighting not to speak. The words won as they tumbled out. "The world doesn't revolve around us. Warren apparently missed that memo."

We were going to need a bigger space, a mediator, and separate rooms for these two because if they clash now, we're so fucked when they got to really know each other. Utterly fucked.

CHAPTER
Sixteen

THEA

I investigated the screen as I talked to a guy with a butterfly tattoo spanning his neck. The tattoo was hot, fucking sexy. But I forced myself to concentrate on the man's eyebrow as he talked. If Warren caught wind that I was even looking at another man, he would flip, and well, I didn't want to ruin the plans. It took me a few days, a few hours daily out in his community that he had built from the ground up, but I'd learned the importance of what we were doing.

And even if I hadn't learned the importance of what he was doing, fuck the united agency. They tried to kill me.

But just because I learned the importance doesn't mean I liked Warren. He was a fucking dick. A fucking dick that I felt an undeniable pull toward. Like, he was a dick, but an attractive one. Not one of those short, stubby dicks, or those unnaturally curved ones. Not one of those with the ugly lumpy tips. But dick perfection, all tall and strong and -

Why was I even thinking about dick and sex right now? It was constantly seeping into my thoughts lately and I was positive it had to be that my body had never been more satisfied in its life and nothing to do with Warren's crazy theory that I was their mate. Maybe my period was coming. That was a solid explanation. I Looked up and tilted my head as I counted down the days from the last cycle date. Oh yeah, it's on the rise and -

"Thea. You're not paying attention!" Warren's voice boomed through the warehouse. "It is imperative that we are all on the same page. I would like to keep everyone here alive, if possible."

I looked around at the three faces watching me. The sudden urge to protect them at all costs tingled through every cell in my body and alerted me I was, in fact, in great danger. Danger of becoming way too fucking attached to these men. I wasn't a protector. I was a killer. A trained killer. A -

"I don't have my camera."

Warren blinked a few times. "Camera." I know it seemed irrelevant, but it was my comfort piece as I went into a mission. Still, he didn't question my need for it, only asked. "Can it be any camera?"

Could it be? Though I was attached to my own, I didn't think any camera mattered. "As long as it instantly prints."

"Rex-" His voice echoed so fucking much through this warehouse and it made me rub my thighs together, causing my body to react.

"On it." Without looking back, Rex walked out the warehouse door and into the night. We were hours away from our plans and nerves hadn't taken over yet. But they would, they always did. Right before I left my place of comfort and breached the walls that surrounded my target, I'd feel my inner self shake with nerves and then I would stifle her. I had no place for nerves when it came to taking a life.

Though, I hoped to avoid taking a life today, the possibility was there.

"Thea-" My name came through the video call again, and I brought my attention back to Rodrick. "This is important."

I locked eyes with him again and felt uncomfortable knowing Warren was so close. "I'm listening."

"It takes three minutes, Thea. Three minutes. No more, no less. Once the drive is in, you have three minutes, and you can't afford to waste them. Anything longer than three minutes and they will know you're into their systems. Anything less and the drive won't fully load. The minute you put that drive into the mainframe, yell time. Warren will start a timer and from there, you will wait."

"Just wait?" That seemed like the potential to be the longest three minutes of my life.

"When it gets to five seconds, count them. Use the Mississippi method if you need to." I smirked, remembering learning that saying the former state equaled one second. "But the moment you hit one second, pull it out."

"If I'm late?"

"There is potential for an explosion." Rodrick said the words casually, but judging by the pulsing vein in his neck, I knew he wasn't joking. This was serious, and I should be both mentally and physically prepared. The United Government would be prepared for things like this. They would be prepared for invasions. It makes sense that they would have a failsafe in place. However, I guess I assumed the failsafe was more like, I don't know, the system crashing. Not the entire room exploding.

"An actual explosion?"

"It was an upgrade made to all the recent facilities." Rodrick leaned back and crossed his arm. "You have the president to thank for that."

Warren cleared his throat as he leaned over the chair I was sitting in. My back was to him, but his sheer size leaning over me engulfed my body and took over the mouse and clicked a few things on the screen. "He knew we were planning to gain some power in the government."

"Why would that matter so much? The government has always been about equal representation." If they weren't, they wouldn't have employed me.

As if he read my mind, Warren said, "It's for appearances. They employed you because you're the best at what you do, and you were fucking moldable. But equal representations were always and will always be appearances. The government will show you and the community what they want you to see. They wouldn't show you the thousands of mutants they are slowly assassinating right under the world's noses."

I wish I believed that they lied. I did. But after years of going through my life, blindly trusting the government only to learn it was fake. Only to learn firsthand that the moment I questioned them in the slightest, they sent their assassins after me. Well, I was no longer blind. I could see clearly and fuck if I didn't want to be part of the change.

I took a deep breath in, letting it out slowly. "Okay then, in three minutes, out. Then what?"

"Then be prepared because they will know you're there Thea, and once they know you're there, there is no stopping their attempts." Rodrick's eyes were hard as he delivered the fact.

"But we will be there too." Warren assured me. "If we get out, and we will, Rodrick's team will take care of the rest of the building."

"Take care, how?"

Deep down, I knew the answer. But the answer just seemed so...vicious. "Once we are in the system, it's all systems, Thea. After that, there is no need for the building or its occupants."

I waited for the sadness to set in. I knew these people. I worked side by side with many of them in trainings and assignments. They had family, children, lives. But that no longer mattered. Their lives did not cancel out the importance of the lives that we had taken all these years. I had done so in ignorance, not knowing the end game. But if any sign of the betrayal of my colleague after just a few questions on mutants was to go by, the fully human beings employed by the United Government knew exactly what they were doing.

Warren's arm wrapped around my shoulder, pulling me back toward his body, offering me a little comfort. "It's a cruel world out there, Doe. And the cruelest monsters always win."

The cruelest monsters always win.

I hated he was right. But no one ever won a dispute by baking cookies unless those cookies were laced with poison. If we wanted to be seen and heard, we needed to show them we would not be snuffed out and that we exist, even when they try to stifle us.

"Get her prepared. We've got two hours." Rodrick shut off the communications, and I found it interesting. He almost gave off the same energy as Warren, but ...

"He's an alpha too." How the fuck did Warren know what I was thinking?

"I can tell." I turned in my chair, directing my attention toward Ansel. "Are you sure you're up for this?"

He pulled a knife from the holster at his hip and flipped it up in the air. Instantly, my heart beat faster. Fear that he would injure himself overwhelmed me and I lunged forward, only to be held in place by Warren's arm. The blade fell from the air in slow motion, and I turned my head, not willing to watch this potentially deadly situation take place.

Warren forced my head back toward Ansel. "Watch."

I held my eyes on him, fighting the urge to close them. The knife came down, spinning handle over blade and right as it neared Ansel, seconds before the velocity of its fall plunged the blade into Ansel's chest... he caught it. By the fucking handle. Like a well-seasoned pro. I would not bother asking why or how that was possible. I've learned that with these men, they make shit happen. And fuck, each time I was always amazed and turned the fuck on by it.

The warehouse door slammed, and Rex appeared, a plastic bag in hand. "It's not the best quality, but it will have to do."

He held out the plastic bag to me and I peered inside. How the hell had he got one of these and the film in that time frame? "They don't even make these any longer. How?"

"I know a guy." He shrugged, and I looked into the bag again.

"A guy who sells Instax? This is..."

Giddiness bubbled inside of me. I've always wanted one of these. I found a vintage advertisement once, and it's been my obsession ever since. "I'll get something better. I just was pressed for time."

"Better?" I stood, so I was closer to his height. "There is nothing better. This is like my childhood dream come true. Do you realize how hard it is to find these?"

His cheeks reddened with a blush and before I thought better of it, I stood on my toes, wrapped my hand around his neck and pulled him down for a kiss. I hadn't meant for it to be anything but chaste. But every single time my lips touched any of these men it's like fire exploded inside of me, heating every space with lust. Never had I experienced such thing and as much as I loved the feel of being on the brink, teetering between bliss and the pain of unfulfillment, I also hated them for it. I hated that my body wanted to depend on their presence when my mind knew I was an independent entity.

Rex's large hand engulfed my hip, as he pulled me into him and damn it, the feel of his hard dick against my stomach had me moaning into his mouth. His fingers threaded into my hair, pulling slightly as he tilted my head back, and I knew I needed to pull away. Now was not the time to be making out when we were hours, minutes, moments away from danger. But then, if now wasn't the time, when was it? It was clear we lived a life that screamed of danger and deceit. Why not take any stolen moment we could?

"We should go." Warren's voice broke into the moment, and I knew he was right. We should go. But damn it, it was hard to tear myself away from Rex.

Rex, though, was more successful. He pulled away, giving me the sexiest little grin before turning to Warren. "I parked the car on the side of the warehouse. It's already fueled."

"Car?" I hadn't ever even seen them use a car, but I guess it made sense. It was in our plan, after all.

"We have vehicles, Doe." Rex laughed. "We just hadn't really needed them."

"What exactly do you need them for?" They went places by foot, which I guess could be because it's harder to track people than vehicles. At least, people that are mutants. A lot of their dealings are underground and when it's not under-ground, it's here in this warehouse. Which brought me to the thought of..."Does it worry you that the United Government knows you are in this place?"

Ansel snorted, clearly finding it amusing. "We travel from time to time to other locations. To have meetings with Rodrick, for instance."

"It doesn't bug us. They know we are here because this is a false location. We only do enough here that we want them to see us. Everything of importance is done elsewhere."

But where is elsewhere then? A place I'd never seen. Had they not trusted me enough yet? I wouldn't be offended if that was the case. I had only been in their lives a few weeks and in that time; I tried to kill them. And they tried to kill me... with so many fucking orgasms, my eyes were nearly permanently crossed from bliss. Fucking Warren and his unnatural cock my body craved. And Ansel and his slow torture. And Rex because fuck him and his after cuddles.

I followed them outside the warehouse, greeting the night with a slow inhale and swift exhale. The night, the shadows. This was my home. I followed them to the side of the ware-house to where a black SUV with black tinted windows sat, waiting. "Who's driving?"

Without missing a beat, both Warren and Rex replied, "Ansel."

Motherfuckers thought they were funny. I mean, it was a little. Except we were on our way to what should be a nearly impossible infiltration that involved sneaking on to a rooftop, Rex blowing up the front door, and me hoping to fucking God that counting the Mississippis didn't do us wrong. I could handle humor, just not when my nerves were shot, and my stomach was rolling around with the fear that today might be the day I lose one of these annoying cling-ons I've gathered.

Ansel's hand touched the front of the car, and, like an expert, he felt along the metal until he reached the handle of the passenger side door and yanked it open. I moved to follow him, heading for the back seat, when Warren's hand wrapped around my wrist, and he yanked me back. His eyes were intense as they hovered over my own, his mouth a breath away as he spoke. "You're scared for us, and you needn't be. We all know the risk of going inside. We only wish you would comply and sit pretty, waiting for us at home."

I licked my lips and his eyes locked onto my tongue. His own tongue darting out to tease against the tip of mine. I swallowed hard. That little movement making my blood boil with need. Fuck. What was wrong with me? "I'd never stay back."

"I know." His teeth nipped at my lip, causing the faintest tinge of metallic mixed with a sting of pain to overwhelm my senses. "It only makes me want you more. When we are done here, I'm going to fuck you so hard, every organ inside of you will be completely and utterly ruined."

"That's..." That's the most disturbing and weird thing

anyone has ever said to me and I had no doubt he intended to do just that. "You've got to work on your romanticism, Warren."

He raised a brow. "That wasn't me being romantic. That was me speaking the truth. Romantic would be me telling you I plan to ruin your organs by fucking you endlessly, but not until you've choked so hard on my cock you've nearly blacked out and my thighs have run red with the blood from your nails digging into my skin as you begged me for air."

The air caught in my lungs, and I fought not to cough or show any reaction to his declaration because that would be like fanning an ember until it burst into flames. Warren wanted to nurture until his distribution grew to be larger than life. If I told him what he demanded of me was the hottest and most erotic thing anyone had ever said to me, he'd only deliver more, and I couldn't have my thoughts be on sex when we were about to risk our lives on a mission I wasn't sure would even work.

"You like that, don't you Doe?" He whispers against my lips. "You'll like it more when my cock is pulsing inside of you. In the car you go, love. We'll be late for the plans."

I turned away from him, my legs shaking with each step I took. The want threatening to overwhelm me, wanting to consume all my senses. I'd never been one to be driven by sex. I could take it, I could leave it. But these men left me wanting to leave nothing. They made me want to claw my way out of a pit to feel them burst inside of me and that, well, was fucking terrifying.

I ducked under Rex's arm and climbed into the backseat. Rex got in after me, shutting the door. The car was silent and when Warren got in, slammed his door, and reached to start the engine, he glanced over his shoulder. "Take care of her, Rex."

Take care of me? Had I read the situation wrong? Was I about to be offed and this whole time I thought these crazy obsessive men wanted my body to worship like their own personal shrine? I looked toward Rex, his face smiling wide as mischief danced in his eyes. "Copy that, alpha."

Alpha? They rarely tossed around those terms unless...

In a blink, Rex had me pushed back against the car door, laying across the seat of the moving vehicle. His body was hovering over mine, his eyes turning to molten lava as he looked down at me. "We have a little time."

"Time?" I swallowed, feeling a lump stuck in my throat.

"Yeah, it's limited, little one."

Did I dare ask? Did I want to know what he was even talking about? "I don't understand."

"We are limited on time to give your body the full working I wish we could. But I'll gladly feast in the time we have."

My core, the traitorous hussy, instantly flooded at his word, my body wanting whatever he wanted to offer. He leaned back on his haunches before taking the waist of my cargo pants and pulling. He didn't bother removing them fully. Only pushing them down enough to allow him to push my knees to the side, allowing room for his body. His fingers went into the lace of my panties and effortlessly, he tore them off, shoving the scrap of material into his pocket.

"I'm keeping these." His voice grew rough. "I'll need a reminder while I'm in there of just what's waiting for me when we're out."

The air brushed against my bare skin and with the slight breeze came the curses of all the men. Warren's voice was strangled, and he demanded again. "Take care of her, Rex."

Rex leaned down, his lips close to mine as he spoke. "He can smell how turned on you are. We all can. It does something to us, jolts us with an unsettling electricity that is only elevated when you're satisfied."

I felt like around these men, I was rarely satisfied. "Then satisfy me."

His chest rumbled at my demand, and he wasted not a

single moment more as he shimmied down my body toward my core. He stopped, hovering over my exposed skin, and inhaled. His eyes closed for a moment before he opened them, staring straight at me as they burned with an intensity I swear I'd only ever seen in Warren. Then, with no more hesitation, he lowered his mouth to my slit and devoured my soul.

Consumed it.

Feasted upon it.

Stole it from my body until I was floating in ecstasy.

It was his tongue. The split tongue was fucking euphoric, and I hated that I waited weeks to feel it against my skin because now that it was running over my slit, teasing my clit, sinking inside of my body and twisting, coaxing me into what is bound to be the most explosive orgasm I've ever experienced, I knew I'd never be able to go back from this. I wanted it. Needed it. I hadn't even peaked, and I craved the feeling all over again.

"Fuck you, Warren." I growled as my chest heaved. He knew what he was doing. He knew that a tongue like Rex's was not a fucking joke and one taste of it would have me coming back for more.

Warren laughed, the sound rich and loud in the car. "Rex must be doing a stand-up job if you're cursing my name."

My eyes rolled upward as my back arched, but Rex's hand clamped down on my stomach, pushing me back down and holding me in place. "I'm going to fucking die."

I groaned the words out as a wave of intense pleasure traveled through me, causing Warren to laugh harder. "Not tonight, Doe. We just want to make sure you understand clearly what you're working toward."

I shifted my hips toward his mouth. "The escalator to heaven. Got it."

My voice was so damn breathless. I pushed one hand against the glass of the window, the other that was clutching the seat released. I let it fall to Rex's hair as I held tightly, pulling it, feeling my orgasm pushing forward. I wanted to fight it, prove to Warren that he couldn't always control me this way, but fuck, Rex's tongue should be illegal. No woman could survive this. No mutants either. Tears were running from my eyes, and it had nothing to do with sadness and everything to do with how fucking intense the buildup was.

I was weak. I knew it. But I couldn't stop my body from cresting over the edge, or my fingers from pulling his hair tight. My hand against the window slipped and slid in the condensation we created and when I opened my mouth for air, the most intense sensation hit me, tearing a scream from my throat. I grappled at anything I could get close to, begging for something to hold me steady. The sound was so damn intense that the glass of the vehicle cracked. The crack spider-webbed downward, splintering the flawless surface.

Rex's hand came up to cover my mouth, while his tongue never left my body. In the distance, I swore I heard Warren curse and I know that Ansel's body was half hanging over the center console as he grabbed onto my fingers. By the time the pleasure faded, my chest was heaving, my throat was raw, and I was positive I wouldn't be able to move another single muscle. Not one. I was as weak as a baby kitten. My bones made of jelly.

The surrounding air was silent. Not a single person dared to speak. Hell, no one moved either. Rex's face was still buried snuggly against my core. I willed myself to pull him up, but even that single move was painful. And I didn't really want him to move. I wanted him to stay exactly where he was for the rest of my life, dishing me out magical oral and making me see other galaxies.

Warren inhaled, the scent of my orgasm no doubt filling the space. He let himself exhale slowly, repeating the process a few times like he was trying to gain control. Then he spoke.

"And that, Thea, is why you'll never be anywhere but at our side."

Yeah, I got it, fucker. You own me, at least my pussy and well, at this second, she had no thoughts of straying anywhere.

CHAPTER
Seventeen

WARREN

Thea's scent still clung to my skin. It surrounded me. It was in every molecule of air I took into my lungs, and I couldn't help but close my eyes against the bliss of it. Rex gave her pleasure under the guise that she needed it, but the truth was, we did. We needed to have the reminder of why we were doing the things we did. Why it was all worth it in the end. Family, unity, love. It was the driving force behind our actions, the desire to be fucking equal. We had it all, to have all these things with her, and I refused to let it slip through our hands.

"You going up with her?" I asked Ansel.

"Yeah. Need a lift, too?" I looked up at the wall. I could climb it, I could glide. If I consumed enough souls, flying would be as fucking easy as pie, but right now, I was driven only on the scent of my mate's pleasure and as invigorating as that was, it wasn't enough to propel me up.

Grudgingly, I admitted I needed help. "Take her up after me."

His head instantly snapped in her direction, following her

scent instead of using the eyes everyone else was graced to have. "You will protect her, won't you?"

What kind of question was that? I'd give up my very own life to make sure she was safe, and I would do it without a moment's hesitation. "I'd die for her. You know that Ansel."

"I do." The words hung heavy in the air, and I sensed there was more.

"But?" I urged him to continue. There was nothing between us, never a single secret, and we would not start now.

"She's changing, Warren."

I looked at her. "Clearly she's changing. She's never been so sexed up in her life. That can be life altering."

"No." His face looked so serious I suddenly paused.

"What do you mean?"

"Can't you smell it?"

I inhaled at his question. I smelled her lust and the remnants of her orgasm. "Her need for us?"

"It's more than that. Her scent is changing, becoming more complex. It's like she's on the verge of..."

I cut him off before he could finish his thought. "Do you think it's possible?"

"Maybe." I trusted him. His senses were heightened more than I could ever dream for mine to be. "There is something else."

I looked at my watch. We have limited time, but still if it was important, I'd let him speak. "What is it?"

"The glass. She shouldn't have been able to do that." He swallowed. "That's something my mutation allows."

"Maybe. Had you asked if she did it before?" Shit, I watched her next to Rex and I swear, after what he did to her, he was her new favorite person. I'd have to work extra hard to get her in my good graces again.

"Warren, you know she hadn't had that power." His voice was low, so she couldn't hear him...

"We don't know much about her."

"We know enough." He paused. "I can smell things changing even when you can't and I'm telling you, keep her safe."

"You don't need to tell me." My voice was hard. Who the fuck did he think he was? I was in charge, not him. "Take me up. I want to be up first while she has Rex on the ground with her."

"Just be careful." He stressed one last time, then his wings sprouted outward, tearing the material of his shirt. He let out a few clicks, feeling out the location of things, grabbed onto me, and shot upward.

I was thankful he made it fast. There was no way to have another man carry you upward without being awkward. He dropped me fast, and I knew he did it to be an ass, letting me hit the wall hard before I slid downward to the ledge. He was gone in an instant and I knew he would bring Thea up shortly and I needed this moment away from her to absorb what he said. I hadn't noticed the change in her scent, but what he is said made sense. She found her mates. She was meant to be with us, and that was a fact I knew from the moment I saw her. Now? We are in uncharted terri-tory, and I wasn't sure what we were supposed to do from here.

I only knew that I wanted her.

And that I would do anything in my power to keep her.

Ansel came into view, his release of our girl so much gentler as he placed her on the ledge, kissing her forehead before he dove down. She looked a little pale as she turned to me. "So, it turns out he has wings."

"Told you as much."

"Telling someone something, and them seeing it for them-selves, are vastly different." She looked over the ledge at Rex and Ansel, no doubt seeing them as they got into position.

"Are you afraid for them?" I asked. She didn't answer for a

long moment, and that was enough of a response. "They are capable."

"I feel..." She sighed. "Ownership."

"You don't like that feeling?" I prodded.

She turned, her body moving fluidly as it navigated the rooftop. "I don't feel like I have a choice. I wanted to pick liking you, not have you tell me I need to and have my body and/or heart just go along with it."

"You are a stubborn one." She pointed to a window, and with little effort, I raised the window upward. "It makes me hot."

"I could sneeze, and you'd get a hard on." She wasn't wrong.

"Do you have everything you need?" I already asked her, but I would ask her time and time again because if we needed to abort, now was the moment to do so.

"This isn't my first time."

"It's not." I agreed. "But it is your first time going against the very agency that trained you. Be aware, they know your moves."

She stopped with one leg inside of the window, her glare was nearly painful as she burned me with her eyes. "You think I don't know that? I'm aware that the people I trusted for years have turned on me and now I'm their target. It's a painful fact, Warren. But life must go on, and in this new life, I get to be the villain they had forced me to be in so many other stories all these years."

"You were never a villain." I offered before gesturing her to keep moving. "No one blames you for doing a job given to you, especially if that job was under false pretenses."

"I blame me." She muttered before she disappeared inside of the building, leaving me to follow behind her.

The attic of the building was dark, dusty, forgotten. The irony of it being just like so many of the mutant's lives who had been forced to flee underground wasn't lost on me. But in the dark, her eyes glowed, and it was a stark reminder that there was always light. We'd find the light for everyone. That was a promise I made myself.

"You're getting ahead of me. Wait a second." I demanded as I tried to fold myself through the window. I didn't want her to take off without me. In fact, I wanted to be in front of her, guarding her from any harm that would come her way. It was my job. Keeping her safe was now my top priority. Equality for our people came second to that.

"No one is going to see me." She looked at me over her shoulder. "Had you forgotten I strive at night?"

I smirked at that. I had not forgotten just how much she could strive in the dark hours. The dark hours were when she was the most compliant. It was the daylight when I got the most resistance from her and her sassy mouth. Without a thought, I snagged a finger into her belt loop and pulled her back into my body. Her back hitting my chest hard, but she didn't turn to look at me. My hand fell to her stomach, pinning her hard against my body.

"I'll never forget how much you strive in the darkness, but it's in the light, when your lips are parted and your breath is fast, that I like watching you most." I traveled my hand lower and for a moment, she didn't fight me. She let my palm skim over her clothes covered body, applying pressure to her most sensitive spots. "After that performance in my vehicle, I fear I have some points to prove, my love. I can't be outdone."

"Of course not." She pushed her ass into my cock. "Heaven forbid if you didn't have the greatest cock and the best mouth. The world would never survive your tantrum."

Cheeky little lady. "You think I have the greatest cock, then?"

"The takeaway here was completely missed." She muttered as my lips skimmed her neck.

"It wasn't missed. I just picked out what was important." I spoke against her skin.

"Yes. Important. Like the fact we are in a government building, ready to commit the ultimate crime and treason... and your fingers are in my pants."

I pulled back and cursed because, damn it, she was right. We were about to commit a serious crime and all I could think about was her screaming my name and having the echo be heard by every man and mutant in a twenty-mile radius. It was how deeply rooted my desire to own her was. I wanted everyone to know who she belonged to so that there would be no question over who lined up against her back to protect her life.

"Tonight then." I promised.

"Tonight." She agreed without hesitation before she stepped forward toward the door. She turned the knob, and I fully expected it to be locked, but by some oversight, it wasn't.

"This door being unlocked and that window being unalarmed is like begging for someone to jump." I commented.

"Or the set up for the perfect murder." She countered. "A single push and bam, a false ruling."

I pursed my lips as I thought about it. "Yeah, that door was definitely left unlocked for a reason."

We slipped through the door and entered a small hallway lined with marble. The whole fucking building was white and grey marble, and it was an eyesore. Why? Why did the government feel the need to flaunt their funds in such an unnecessary way? It was funds that could have gone to supporting programs that helped my kind, instead of all the effort they went through to hinder them.

Thea's feet were silent as they touched the marble, her body pulling the shadows toward her naturally, obscuring my view of her. It came naturally to her. The ability to sneak in, assassinate, and get out was a skill she honed in on over the years, and now, even with me following her through the building, she used that skill as second nature.

"You're stepping too loud." She hissed as we reached a set of stairs leading to the second floor. The second floor was our desired location, but far riskier to be on. It was a floor of balconies, opening up to the ground below, overlooking the main lobby.

"I'm stepping the only way I know how." I shot back harshly, my whisper less than quiet. "You try lugging around a body this size and see how you step. Not everyone is a trained killer."

She had the nerve to look me directly in the eye before letting her eyes roll. "You could at least try to be quiet. Some of us would like to get in and out without confrontation. Not everyone prefers brutality up front."

"If brutality gets the job done." I kept my voice low as we stepped down the stairs.

"Men and their egos." She turned to me, holding her finger up to her lips to quiet me. Convenient that she decides I need to be quiet when I wanted to say every damn thing to defend myself.

Footsteps traveled over the marble in the hall we were about to enter. We froze, though we both knew no one could see us as we descended. The stairs were closed in and only the point of exit was visible from the hall. Still, we had no clue what direction the steps were headed and if they went up, we were fucked.

The steps continued past the stairs, and I let go of a breath I hadn't realized I was holding. The tension in my body remained though, reminding me that as much as I wanted to flirt and banter with the vixen in front of me, now was not the time. As much as I wanted to push her to the side and lead, she was in charge here. She knew the layout. She knew where we were going without a single mistake of movement and I?

Well, I'd never stepped foot into this marble monstrosity until now and I was shit at direction.

She traveled slowly down the remaining steps, before covering her whole body in the shadows and peaking outward. I knew no one could see her, but damn it, I was so utterly aware of her presence. She'd never be able to hide from me, even if she tried. I would track her down, swim through the inkiest of blacks, and still gather her to my body. She had no escape. I'd never let her free and maybe that seems obsessive. But I know she's mine. I'm just waiting for her to fully realize it.

"It's empty." She stepped forward onto the marble floor. "Step light. There's no room for barbarians in this building."

If she was trying to insult me, she didn't do a good job at it. We were barbaric, but barbaric gets shit done. No one ever accomplished anything by sending flowers and hoping for favors. Especially when blood, guts, and egos are involved. Barbaric actions got noticed, it pushed forth actions and in the end, it brought forth outcomes. There was nothing to be ashamed of about that.

Still, I followed her advice and walked as silently as possible, damn near tiptoeing through the hall as I followed her. I resisted the urge to look over the rail, trying to stay against the wall and out of view, but I wonder if my boys had entered the building yet. If they had, they had gone unnoticed. It wouldn't be long, and I knew that chaos would swiftly follow.

She slinked forward and more footsteps echoed on the marble from the other side of the hall. She looked around frantically, but there was no place to hide. We needed to get to the door from where the footsteps sounded, and we couldn't cross paths without going unnoticed. "Wrap me in your shadows."

"I can't." She hissed.

"You can." I ordered. "Fucking do it."

She turned to me, her eyes so illuminating that I couldn't figure out how none of the humans saw her in this state. "I don't know how Warren."

"Figure it out." I had faith in her. She could do fucking anything if she tried hard enough.

"Now is not the time for trial and error." Her voice was panicked.

"Then don't have an error. What other choice do we have, Thea?" I hated putting the pressure on her like this, but she knew going into it that there was a likely chance that she would have to try and maybe she forgot. But I didn't. She was my partner, both on this mission and now in life, and part of having a partner was to push them to their full potential.

"It's not that simple."

"It is." The steps grew louder. "They are getting closer."

She cursed but didn't waste a single breath on arguing further. Her fingers grabbed onto my shirt as she pulled me toward her, then she pushed me against the wall. I towered over her in height, her body so much smaller than I was. Still, she closed her eyes as she pushed up against me, forcing my back hard into the wall. Then she tilted her head down, burying her face into the material of my shirt.

At first, nothing happened. Then, my skin chilled as the cool shadows seeped toward us. They were nothing like I thought as they coated my skin. They were damp and moving, like a thousand tiny fingers constantly touching my body. The feeling stole my breath and made me shiver from the chill, but her body heat seeped into my skin, blocking out the feel of frost. Was this what she felt like every time? The feeling of fingers snuck up my neck, crawling over my frame until it covered me, leaving my vision in a haze of grey.

And it was then that I knew she had done it. She had pulled her power, stretching, and morphing it, allowing it to lend me protection. My chest swelled with pride under the heat of her body and my hand went to her hip, holding her tight against me. The footsteps grew louder, pounding against the marble and all I wanted to do was keep her close, make sure our bodies were aligned tightly together because the irrational part of my mind had me convinced that if we were flush in the shadows of the ill lit building, it would make us completely invisible to all eyes should the shadows fail us.

Though I doubted they would fail us. I had confidence in her. I just ... fuck. My heart was beating so damn fast I wondered if she could hear the blood flow in and out of every chamber. My mouth felt dry as the steps grew impossibly close and I knew in seconds they would turn the corner and we'd be seen or we'd be invisible to their eye and though I knew the shadows danced around me in a thick cloud, it didn't soothe the anxiety that we might be discovered. Her body shifted against mine, her back going rigid, and I swore I heard her faintly whisper, *relax*.

I couldn't relax. Not knowing the danger she could potentially be in. She proved at her apartment that she was more than capable of caring for herself, but that didn't soothe the animal inside of me, the beast who wanted to protect their mate. She could protect herself, but I'd be damned if I let her willingly do so. Not now that I'd claimed her as my own and my soul is mended together with hers.

I wonder if she could feel it? Feel the string that tied us together.

The man and the woman turned the corner, chatting, a stack of papers in hand. The woman glanced toward us, then looked away and she continued her chat. They kept walking. The heels of her stilettos clicked, echoing obnoxiously loud through the vaulted ceilings. We stayed frozen, waiting until the clicks of the steps faded. A door opened and slammed shut in the distance, signaling they were no longer a threat.

Not like they were a threat prior. Only a nuisance.

She didn't pull away from me as the door slammed and when I looked down toward her, her bright eyes were staring up at me. My heart stuttered for a moment. I forgot to breathe. My chest felt heavy as it begged me for the need of air. Still, I didn't move. I dared not break the spell on us. She shuttered with a deep breath that she inhaled, before standing on her toes and kissing my jaw.

No other gesture was exchanged before she pushed away from my body. "It's around that bend and halfway down."

She walked confidently away and for a few long moments, I forgot to follow. All at once, the objective came back to me and I forced my feet forward, urging myself to move even when I wished to pull her back into the shadows to have her close and protected.

We reached the door, and she jiggled the handle. "Locked."

Of course, it would be fucking locked. It was their primary system. "Rodrick will deactivate all log ins right about ..." I glanced at my watch. "Now."

As if on cue, the keycard system blinked on and off, showing an error message. The only issue we had to worry about now was the door. The door, which apparently wasn't an issue at all, as Thea dropped to her knees and pulled out some thin equipment I hadn't seen before. She began working the lock, looking seriously like the sexiest thing in existence.

Naturally, she would know how to pick a lock. Why wouldn't she? She excelled at everything else while I was planning to just break down the door.

There was a faint click, and she paused, a smile curling the corners of her lips before she looked up at me. While maintaining eye contact, she twisted the knob, the door popped open effortlessly. "We're in."

CHAPTER
Eighteen

REX

I stood outside the building, hiding against a nearby building, until I watched both Thea and Warren disappear through the window. It was hard parting ways. I wanted to wrap my body around hers and carry her back to our place, to show her the comfort and affection she so clearly deserved. I wanted to keep her close to me. To savor every flavor on her skin.

There were so many things I wanted to do and all I could do was watch her disappear through the damn window.

It was for the best, I knew that. But I still tasted her on my lips. Still smelled her scent every time I inhaled like it was now officially embedded into my DNA. Warren was right, not that I doubted him. But after we had a taste of her, there was no going back for us. She was it. She was our official, undeniable mate. Even if we hadn't made it completely official yet. We would when the time was right.

I questioned the theory at first because if there was a

single female out there that could produce any child of a mutant, we'd never find her. But here we are, our fingers touching her skin, our mouth against hers and you cannot convince me that the heavens made her for anyone else but us.

"Are you planning to go inside or just sit here and stare at the sky?" Ansel asked as he landed a few feet away from me.

"I haven't decided yet." I admitted.

"It's all so fascinating, isn't it?" He sighed. "She's ours. I can smell the difference in her. Everything is changing."

Everything was changing, and that was terrifying. "Do you think-"

"It's too soon to tell if it's even possible." He cut me off.

Fuck, I wanted the impossible to be possible, at least this once. I wanted theories to be true and to hold the proof in my hands. We were a bunch of misfits. Society's outcasts. But damn if we didn't form the perfect bond of a family.

"We need to get into position." He reminded me.

He was right, I'd almost forgotten. He disappeared into the night, finding his place where he would be unseen. And I? I shifted my skin to match my surroundings, blending myself in with the green of the grass and the white of the painted brick. You wouldn't see me unless you were up close or looking, but by then, it would be too late.

I slunk along the building, my feet stepping light on the grass and pebbles, trying to not make a sound as I crept closer to the door. I knew it would be locked. Few people were here after hours, and the ones who were, had picked an unfortunate profession because there was no way, not in this lifetime, that Ansel or Warren would let a human live. Me? I'm softer than they are, but I know my purpose now and I won't let anyone disturb it.

I heard Ansel's click. He was above me, crouched on the roof, waiting to fly downward. He needed the signal, a signal that wasn't exactly discrete when you have such high-powered hearing as he did. I crept closer to the door, stopping only feet away from it. Blending, I reached forward, shaking the handle. Locked, like I knew it would be, but it wasn't a worry. How quick could glass doors be opened when faced with destruction?

The answer was seconds.

I reached into my pocket and pulled out some explosive putty, some concoction someone from Rodrick's team came up with. It was a weak charge, they said, causing silent but high-powered charging to shake through the glass until it eroded at the edges, efficiently breaking the lock right off the doors. It worked for windows too, though I'd not experimented there. After working the putty in my fingers until it was soft enough, I plastered it along the door's edge, pressing it down until it stuck against the glass.

Then I waited.

The molecules in the putty meshed and bound and less than a minute later, I could already feel the heat radiating off it as they reacted to each other. I placed my hand on the glass, feeling it shimmy slightly under my touch. The slight vibration travelled up my arm, and I knew that the creation was doing its job.

Before my eyes, shards of glass slipped off the door, each one falling solo as it hit the floor, preventing the telltale sign of a crash. I waited until the whole edge was gone, then I jiggled the door. The lock gave easily, having nothing to hold on to, to force the mechanisms in place and secure it. I pushed the door open, my feet crunching slightly on the glass as I walked through.

In seconds, Ansel was at my side, his whispered voice breaking into the surrounding silence. "That was most effective."

"I'd like it in bulk. I'm impressed."

We talked no further, knowing full well that it was about to get a little dicey. We were almost fully into the center of the lobby when we were first noticed. It was a single guard by a desk, though I knew they held so many more threats in the building. Even at night, they were well secured. They had to be. The threat of mutants was apparently high to them. As it should be, now that they created the problem between mutants and humans themselves. They feared retaliation. What they should fear was retribution. We weren't here to return an act of wrong. We wanted vengeance for our people.

"Do you have a pass?" The guard asked, not even bothering to get up. Maybe he figured with the door locked, we had a key or an escort. You would have thought he would have been more concerned.

"I don't need a pass." Ansel answered, his cane bumping against the desk.

It was distracting, I knew. People saw him and got uncomfortable. The thought of someone with a disability and the possibility that they would have to step out of their comfort zone for one second to assist always made people squeamish. Only, nothing about Ansel was requiring help. He could perfectly maneuver himself through this life.

The guard looked between us, his posture screamed of his discomfort. "I'm sorry, sir. Everyone who enters this building needs to have a pass or a keycard."

Ansel, the smartass he was, cleared his throat. "Sir, if I didn't have a keycard, how do you think I got into this building?"

One beat. Two Beats. Three...

The guard slowly reached for his radio while his other hand was reaching for an alarm button. He could press it. Fuck, I'd help him. I leaned over, making sure he got a full view of the scales that shimmered on my neck before I pressed the button myself. An alarm instantly blared, but the man didn't live long enough to hear it. Ansel reached forward, his nails extending into claws like a bat, before he tore through the man's throat, ripping out his vocal cords, tearing his throat to shreds, letting all his blood pump out of him and drip down his pristinely white uniform shirt.

It was a slow and painful death for sure, but had it been us that were on our deathbeds, they would have made it slow, too. Only, it would involve more torture and less care for the basics of humanity. He tried to gasp as he grabbed at his throat, trying to stop the flow of blood, but there would be no stopping it and as his glassy eyes watched us, I knew he understood that fact.

"Disconnect." Ansel's voice broke into my thoughts, reminding me it has to be this way.

I was a softy, and he knew it. Another second or two of watching him die and I would have wanted to aid in his survival. But there needed to be death if we were going to bring new life into the existence of the mutants. Unfortunately, this was the job he signed up for.

Footsteps pounded down the hall, a parade of people heading this way, and I knew we were outnumbered, though that fact didn't scare me any. We've got this. We've got this. "We've got this."

"I've no doubt. We need three minutes. They are in." When he told me they were inside, I knew not to question it. His hearing could pick up the smallest of detail, the furthest of conversations, pretty much anything a human wouldn't want known, he could hear from further than a football field. It came in handy, though sometimes he was impossible to be around.

Every guard in the building burst through the same door all at once, nearly stumbling over each other's feet to make it through the narrow passage. "Were they all on lunch?"

Ansel smirked, but said nothing as he stepped aside,

letting them all take in their fallen coworker. The registering of what they witnessed was delayed, each one trying to piece together the gore in front of them and relate it to the face that was slumped over it. Then there were gasps before a single person raised a weapon.

A fire rang out, missing.

But it was all we needed to spring into action and begin what would be the end of this government facility.

"We have backup coming." The shout echoed through the room, bouncing off the unnaturally high ceilings as it ricocheted back at us. We'd known they would call for reinforcements, but all that mattered was we got done before their spares came barreling into the building. But we didn't know how far out they were, never predicted their location because even Thea didn't know where they boarded. She could never board in the facility.

The reason was utterly clear to her now.

The first man to reach me wasn't prepared for the strength behind my normal cool demeanor. He raised his gun and without a thought I grabbed onto the barrel, bending the metal upward, rendering the weapon useless. He was forced to abandon it, leaving only his fists and a knife at his waist that he never had time to release.

His first swing was his only mistake. Not only was the form shit, but I caught the fist midair, twisting it back until I heard a series of snaps that ripped a scream from his throat. I let go. The arm fell limp to his side. I gave him no time to recover. Taking the knife Thea gave me, I savored the weight of the handle for a moment then I jammed it into his abdomen, before pressing the lever that injected his body with a burst of CO_2. The burst of pure oxygen was like an explosion to his organ, and the man dropped hard.

I pulled the knife from his body, wiping the blood away as I squeezed the handle tight. Never had I been more in love with a woman than this moment, as I used her knife to kill an enemy. Fuck, I loved her.

I squeezed the handle one more time, my eyes leveled with a ferocity that was more feral, more Warren, more deadly, than I'd ever had.

"Who's next?"

CHAPTER
Nineteen

THEA

The lock gave way easily, with minimal effort. Without a keycard requirement, their security was lacking. Still, it only took moments for the lock to give way, my tool working it like softened butter, sliding right past the mechanisms to open the door. I let the door fall open before I stood and, as I stepped a foot inside the room, Warren pulled me back.

His lips were against mine in an instant, his kiss hard and quick as he muttered against my skin. "I've never wanted to bend you over a rail more than when I watched you pick that lock."

I fought not to laugh. Doing so would give us away. "Lies, always full of lies."

There was absolutely no situation that Warren didn't want to bend me over somewhere and make me beg to cum. He was good at it, too. My core was already soaked just from the thought. But I needed to focus. A task was hard to do when the man I was partnered with smelled so fucking divine. Toss in his attention span, which I swore was that of a hamster, and productivity was hard to achieve.

I pushed away from him. My mind and body remembered what it was like to be so close to him while my shadows encompassed us. A shiver ran down my spine. He was so fucking confident I could do it, and I did it. But the way it felt inside our secret little bubble, the tingles of our skin as the darkness danced against us, made me nearly weak. I wanted to take him right there against the wall and I fucking despised that fact because I kept telling myself I hated him.

And I did hate him.

But I also was undeniably drawn to him, and it made me furious.

I wanted him. I hated him. The emotions were, well, complicated.

Commotion below broke out and Warren's body stiffened. "We need to hurry."

It was easy for him to say, his body wasn't on fire for a man he hated. Or woman. Whatever he desired, I guess. Did he and the boys partake in that type of activity?

I nodded once, slipping into the room while he stood guard in the hall. Dropping to the floor, I crawled around, finding a large slot between two oversized machines. I removed the drive from my pocket before reaching my hand through the space. My arm barely fit. The boys never would have managed. I searched around with my fingers, knowing I had one chance to get this right. When my fingers found the slot it was looking for, I wasted no time shimming the drive from my palm to my fingers and shoving it into the mainframe.

"It's in."

Warren's head peaked into the room as I was pulling my arm back. "Good. Because the chaos has started."

The thought of what was happening below made my heart beat in overdrive. I didn't know them long, but I felt a possessiveness and the thought of danger didn't sit right with me. I knew they could protect themselves. In fact, the limited action I've seen proved that their abilities far exceeded any human's. But I didn't have eyes on them. I could not watch them conquer their challenges as I laid on the floor in this computer room.

The computer in front of me blinked and a screen I hadn't even known existed blinked to life.

In front of me, the screen took on a life of its own and I could only assume Rodrick had everything to do with it because I was completely lost in what was happening. I was only good at typing out an email and inserting the drive. But as the computer moved from screen to screen, codes appeared, then disappeared. Images flashed. I knew that whatever was happening was big. It was the difference between going on to the next step of our journey blind or going in fully prepared.

"Is it almost done?" Warren's voice was antsy.

"It's been like thirty seconds." He should know. He had the watch and timer going.

"Fuck." He wheezed out the words. "I hear steps coming."

My heart pounded into my ribcage. There was nothing I could do unless they wanted a failed mission. "Get inside."

I made the order without thinking because he was the distraction. But he was also a wall of defense until this job was done. If they were slow on their discovery of him, then that bought us a few extra moments. However, it made it harder for him to defend us if he was backed into a corner of the room.

"That's not a good idea." He muttered.

"We need extra time." I demanded, as I watched the codes flutter on the screen. "Get inside and close the door."

His eyes met mine, speaking things I hadn't learned to read just yet. "It will buy seconds, but it could cost us our live."

"What is worth more?" I growled.

His eyes glanced back at the hallway. "The outcome of this information is worth more than my life."

"Then come in."

"But nothing is worth the cost of yours." He stepped full out of the doorway, shutting the door to his back.

"Warren." I growled his name, but the door didn't open. "Damn it, Warren."

The footsteps in the distance grew louder, and I knew any second, they would see him, and I feared not for him, but for them. I'd seen what he could do without lifting a finger and I worried how many lives he would take to save my single one. Would it be worth it? Would his own soul suffer and blacken to chars with each life he drained?

A beep from the mainframe caused my head to turn, remembering that fucking Warren had the stopwatch. Of course he did. I crept toward the door, listening for any sound on the outside. Nothing yet. Warren was silent. That could be a good sign. Maybe they didn't pass this direction, and they were too preoccupied with the battle I heard raging below. But then there was a shout and a thunder of footsteps pounded against the marble floor.

He'd been spotted. I knew without even cracking the door. I felt his power gather, the air crackled with its energy and even through the thick wood dividing us, I could hear bodies fall.

"Thirty seconds, Thea." He grunted from the other side, and I knew it was consuming a shit ton of energy holding them off.

I scrambled toward the computer, ready to dive in and steal the drive. "Come on. Come on."

The commotion outside grew louder, the chaos no longer contained. I feared what I'd find when I opened the door.

"Twenty-five." Warren's voice made me anxious. I wanted to run to the door, throw it open and help him. I palmed my blade at my thigh, itching to remove it. I could help him. I could ease some of the tension I felt straining inside of him from here. I could-

"Twenty."

Jesus, his counting was making me shake with nervousness. I knew we were running the time down. I nearly thrummed with the anticipation of hitting that last five seconds. It couldn't be wrong. The count couldn't be off. I needed to get this right.

"Fifteen."

"Warren. How bad is it out there?" I could help him, even if it was flinging this knife through the room and gutting someone from twenty meters away.

"It's nothing. Easy. I've got it." I heard a grunt and for a second, I thought I felt pain shoot through my side. "Ten seconds."

Ten seconds. We've got ten seconds. All I needed to do was crawl on the ground, get into position and be ready to take over and help the second this drive was in my hand. That was assuming I didn't blow up the place. Blowing up the place was highly likely. As if my thoughts aligned, there was an explosion, and the building rocked, sliding me back against the wall. It had to be Rex. I knew he got a shit ton of toys from Rodrick recently and I imagined that to be one of them. There was no way agents would actively try to destroy government property.

I thought as I, an agent, tried to hack their systems.

"Five. Seconds." There was a growl on the other side of the door, and I couldn't examine the ferocity of it. Not when I had to count. Not when I had to get every second correct.

Five Mississippi.

The floor rumbled.

Four Mississippi.

A human wailed.

Three Mississippi.

The sound of bones crushing echoed through the noise.

Two Mississippi.

Chains rattled as foots pounded down.

One Mississippi.

I reached forward, closing my eyes as I took hold of the drive and pulled.

The surrounding room went silent for a moment. Everything seemed to freeze. Then, like I was stepping out of a soundproof tunnel, the chaos that reigned on the other side of the door rushed back in, slamming into my senses. I jumped up, shoving the flash drive into my pocket, and rushed to the door. I threw the door open and before I could stop the sound from leaving me, a wail escaped my lips.

CHAPTER
Twenty

ANSEL

It was a well-known fact that people underestimated the blind. It was their fault for not seeing the potential. Ha, seeing. You would think that with their ability to see would come some logic. I've adapted, I've heightened my senses, I've learned to navigate a world without light when all they do is seek and reach for it. I didn't need the light to guide me. I had the drive to move forward, anyway.

They aimed for Rex, viewing him as the threat. They were completely blind to the fact that I was far more threatening than Rex ever would be. But I let them aim for whatever target they wished and when their backs were turned, I struck. Like lightening hitting a tree, my movements and target never known. They hadn't predicted I was dangerous, and that was their cause of death.

I struck at their back, aiming straight for their kidneys, and they went down hard, their voices drowned out by the commotion as they screamed. It took me years to hone the skill, years to learn what would kill and where to strike. Years that were well worth it.

The flood of men that entered the lobby was impressive. It was like they had suspected an attack would come and they waited, buying time until we showed. But really, are two men against their hoards really an attack? We were outnumbered. Smart of them to overestimate our capabilities. Dumb of them to not realize that their estimate was still not sufficient.

I kept track of Rex, my mind and body so in tune to his, as it had been for nearly half my life. I didn't need my eyes to know where he'd be. I could almost feel his movements, like it were my own. We were one, born of necessity and held together by joint animosity. The humans never stood a chance.

"You need one of these knifes." Rex panted as he met me at my side. I could smell the blood that dripped off him, the metallic scent delicious and alluring.

"I'll leave the fun toys to you." I gripped my weapon tighter. The sound of a bullet whizzing in our direction had me pushing him to the left. "I can handle a regular knife just fine."

"You literally have the biggest dick I've ever seen." He laughed as I ducked a bullet aimed at my head. "Fucking fearless."

The world does not move when it lets fear stand in its way.

The material of Rex's clothes rustled, and I knew he was pulling something out of his pocket. "Should we try this?"

"I literally don't know what this means." I grunted as a man swung for me, grazing my cheek a little. It was a lucky swing that ended the moment my weapon jutted forward, piercing directly into his heart. I felt the impact, then pushed the weight of my body into it. The knife pushed through the flesh and cracked through the bones until it was fully emerged, leaving only the hilt. I pulled it out, having to push against the man's chest to dislodge my knife.

"This ball thing Rodrick sent." He clarified.

If it was from Rodrick, it will be a good time. "Try away."

I heard a twisted sound indicating he did just that. The faintest of clicks came from Rex's hand. "Throw it!"

I made the demand just in time. Mere seconds after leaving Rex's fingers, the tiny ball he had held exploded with such force that the ground rocked below our feet and debris spattered in every direction. "That was an arm."

He sounded nauseous as he spoke. But we didn't have time for him to be weak. Weakness was for the dead, and we were anything but close to death. I heard a grunt and my ears tilted upward, hearing rows of men heading toward Warren, both sides of him about to be surrounded. "They were prepared, Rex. They knew we were coming."

An internal leak.

I couldn't fathom who. I trusted the men and woman I came into this building with, literally with my life. I trusted Rodrick nearly as much. But somehow, they knew we were coming tonight. That's the only way they would have had this many men waiting to attack. The question was who? And how much did they know? Did they know we were already in their systems? Did they care? Was the risk of national security worth the capture and death of Warren?

He was wanted. We knew. It wasn't just at a local level. It was national. The stakes were high. They were fucking insanely high, but worth the risk of association.

"We need to go up." Down here was dying down. The bodies were no doubt greater numbers than the lives.

No sooner did the words leave my mouth than a wail filled the air, echoing. "Thea!"

We no longer cared about the men still left. Our senses drove us upward, stumbling on the stairs to get to her. Warren was one thing. Though we cared for him, he was strong enough and capable enough to save himself. But Thea? Our hearts and souls would not let us leave her to fend for herself against men determined to bring her destruction. We reached the top, and I paused, letting my senses find her.

I didn't hesitate after that. I tore through people, not caring who met the blade of my knife. Beside me, Rex did the same and in front of us, the horror of chains jingled as Warren fought for his freedom. There were so many, so fucking many bodies that I couldn't figure out how they stayed contained in the narrow hall. I used the narrow space to my advantage, showing no hesitation as I pushed men over the rail.

Their screams echoed until their body was stopped by the marble below, a sickening wet crunch as their skulls split open on the hard ground. They could survive that fall, though I doubt any of them did, and if they had, they would no longer be a threat to us. Every bone needed to walk up those stairs was likely broken and unless they were mutant, there would be no getting past that.

A roar broke free from Warren, and I could feel the tension in the air. I could feel the shift. I feared it. If Warren let his full self release into this world, there may be no going back. Each time he's pushed to the edge, it became harder to bring him back to lucidity. This could be it. This could be the last time and we could lose him. Would it be the end for us? Maybe. Though I knew we could push on without him, it wouldn't be the same.

Thea screamed, and though I heard her fighting, I knew she was overwhelmed by the numbers. She didn't understand yet that we would do anything for her. Face anything. We would fight to the end, or we would all go down together. The air shifted against my skin, tiny pricks of ice rubbed against my body, and I felt it, felt the darkness creep around me in the oddest sensations. Felt the moment the darkness wrapped around my skin and pulled me in a direction.

I went willingly.

I only knew darkness, never light, and I'd walk willingly into an abyss if it called my name seductively.

The pull was toward Thea, and for the first time since she came into our life, I wished I could see around me. See her. See what had her scared so damn bad that her shadows reached for us in comfort even as her knives plunged into the hearts of those who'd wronged her? Another chain rattled, the sound so loud in a place filled with the screams of pain and the scent of death.

An arm swung at me. I caught it midair and just when I was about to retaliate, the body of the man went limp, his soul sucking from inside as Warren called it to him. This was bad, so fucking bad. The more souls he ate, the more he consumed inside of him, the more tempted his beast was to come out and play.

A roar sliced through the room. Agony tinged the sound, and the flooring under our feet rattled.

It was too late, they had pushed too far. If they hadn't touched her, if they had kept their hands off her. Maybe, just maybe, he would have let them live.

CHAPTER
Twenty-One

THEA

I threw open the door, and instantly my stomach sank. I hadn't realized a sound left my mouth until it was too late, but I was thankful that it had. It drew some of the attention away from Warren, took some of the attention away from wrapping him in chains and directed it towards me. They were heartless, that was for sure. They didn't care that the metal they wound around his neck was pulling tight, cutting into his skin, and causing angry red welts. And if they didn't care about someone that I cared about, then I couldn't return the favor.

My knife left my hand before I thought better of it, sinking into the side of the head of the man controlling the chains, hitting his ear like it was a target. I felt the pull of Rex and Ansel, knowing they would come to my aid as I reached for a blade in my boot, wasting no time tearing into everyone who got near me. There were tons of them, and for the first time, I wondered if we could pull this off. This amount of people in the facility wasn't normal. They knew we were coming. They had to have known.

How?

I shuddered at the thought of how they got that knowledge because it made me question who we could trust and who we couldn't. How far did the friendship of Warren run between his men and his community that someone would tip off the government? They wanted him. It was abundantly clear that in his mass of destruction and fading life, that he was the main target. The bodies that surrounded him were victims of his power, and the souls that now danced inside of him only seemed to fuel his strength.

His neck bulged as he tore at the chains, snapping them off his body and throwing them at the men that were so eager to take him down. The chains crashed into a person, the weight of them pushing him over the ledge and down into the lobby. I tried not to cringe, knowing his fate. He deserved it. They all deserved it. But that didn't make it easy to stomach.

I tried to compartmentalize what I was doing and what had to be done. It was so much easier to be given a file and told of an atrocious crime they had committed and think that removing them from this universe was an actual favor to humanity. But this? This was a mass scale of blood, and it was wrong. Maybe it was wrong because it was needless. These people were following orders, but if they knew the truth behind the orders, would they still blindly go to their deaths?

A bullet whizzed past me, and I swore I heard it coming, dodging to the left and barely missing the impact of it. Warren roared his anger, veins in his forehead bulged as he inhaled, floating the line of men's souls who stood nearest to him through the air and into his body. They were so damn faint. An illusion of the eye, an iridescent glimmer in midair. Then they were gone. Consumed as his face morphed into bone and a haze swarmed around him.

I swung my blade as Rex and Ansel appeared, their faces a relief but also a worry. They were helping, and I appreciated it. But how could I watch them all at once, hope for all their safety, when I was distracted by all that was around me? Ansel didn't delay in his movements, he dove right in, not caring that he had no clue who was close and what weapon they held that gave them the advantage.

I couldn't keep watching them though, not when they assured me repeatedly that they could care for themselves. Not when the flood of people out to kill us, kept coming. Not when I just needed to struggle to survive. If we got out of this, I might kill these boys myself. I wasn't prepared. I'd never had this many people against me before and sure, I was trained for this. A fucking professional. But I was fighting against the very people who trained me. The United Government never feared me. They were a part of everything I've done over a huge part of my life, and they felt no threat from my existence.

It's because you were valuable to be used, a voice inside of my head repeated.

It was true, I had been used. Used to kill innocent mutants. Used to do the dirty work that the government didn't want on their own hands. I had all the photos to prove it. Every single one. Every single face. I memorized. I knew their names. Their occupation. Their age. I'd killed them needlessly.

From behind, a man approached Warren and without thinking my shadows reached out, pushing against the man in its attempt to shield and protect Warren. But he was too far away, and I hadn't figured out how to reach the distance. I stepped away from the safety of the wall at my back, stepped away from the protection I needed and pushed harder in the direction, no longer using my shadows to hide, but using them to fight. My shadow wrapped around the wrist of the man, and I closed my eyes, envisioning every tiny tick of a movement that he made, then I yanked my shadow back.

The man dragged along the floor screaming as the unseen forces held on to him, pulling him toward me. He fought. He tried to escape. He scraped and scratched and pulled at his own flesh, but you can't escape the unseen. Once it takes you in its grasp, you have no way out. The shadows stopped at my feet, delivering him to me like a gift, and I wasted no time plunging my knife into his heart. I didn't regret it. Not when I had to weigh the consequences. His life or Warren's.

I fucking hated Warren. But he was mine and if anyone was going to stab him in the back, I'd like it to be me and probably before he slams me against the wall and fucks me until I'm mindless.

Another pull of the darkness dragged a man toward me by his feet, his belly scraping against the ground as his fingers clawed into the floor. He reached for people, trying to grab their ankles to stop the pull, but it did no good. He was the target. He who dared to nick Warren's flawless skin. He screamed and begged as he traveled along the floor. It was pointless. My heart had no mercy toward him, just like his heart would have shown no mercy toward us.

It was ironic. They were human. Yet, they were more robotic and controlled than mutants would ever be. Maybe that's why they wanted us dead. Our minds were free. We were far less of a threat dead than we were alive. They made a mistake, though. By not ending us in the beginning but thinking they would alter the injections a little and things would be fine, they allowed us to grow in numbers and gather in strength. The humans created the problem they now sought to eliminate, but they lacked the strength, even in numbers, to get the job done.

The shadow pull stopped at my feet, the man crashing into my boots, as he attempted to twist his body to look up toward me. I shifted my knife from one hand to the next and when I plunged it down into the flesh, finding a perfect spot between two ribs, somehow avoiding all bone, I blinked. For a moment, I swore my fingers were completely bone. A flash of a skeletal structure before it was replaced by my familiar flesh.

I inhaled. The very air that kept me alive, nearly choking me as I gasped around it, trying not to cough.

Impossible.

But was it? My eyes had never done me wrong and now? Now I was suddenly questioning everything.

The surrounding darkness stretched, allowing me not to ponder how insanely different this was. Like Warren had opened the Pandora's box himself, allowing my shadows to hide him had given him full control. A control I hadn't even known was possible. And now? Now they were like a familiar friend, assisting me in my path to triumph instead of hiding me from view.

I stepped over the body, another step away from the familiar wall at my back. Another step away from the safest position in the room. My mind was blurred, and a jumbled mess. My heart reached for the three men I somehow attached myself to. Each of them fighting for their own survival. Each of them giving back twice as hard as the fight was giving them.

Rex reached into his pocket, pulling a cube out. Pressing a button, he tossed it. Gold smoke rose, the hauntingly beautiful color reminding me of a flower, bright and bold. Yet stark and deadly. It drew people in, the color vibrant, leaving them unaware of the poison it held inside its petals. A sunflower? A rose? A carnation of death? Everyone watched the color rise, the waves of smoke forming curves and angles.

It was Ansel who realized its purpose. Just a distraction. He stepped forward as people watched, not caring that it was lives he touched and took as he reached around their throat from behind, slitting their throat, letting them fall to the floor as their air gurgled through the blood that was flooding their airways.

Below glass broke. The sound forced their attention to turn away. "Backup."

The declaration from one of the few men remaining made Warren curse. His growl of anger filling the space before he stepped forward, using a claw I hadn't known he even possessed to sever the man's head from his body. The head fell to the floor, rolling slightly before coming to a stop. I gagged, the image something I'd never forget.

Warren looked bigger, larger, stronger. His face structure was more defined as the skin pulled tight against bone. His muscles bulging and tearing at his shirt sleeves as he stalked his next prey. I looked down at the piles of humans who had never made it to see tomorrow. Had he eaten the souls of all the dead, or just the ones whose life he had sucked straight from their body and drunk down like a shot of vodka?

Footsteps thundered against the marble steps as their backup arrived, too late for them to live. Ansel and Rex turned, ready to face the new fight head on, ready to win. My bones were exhausted as I moved forward, and I wondered how much longer we could fight and stay on top of it. How much longer could we win when their people were endless and disposable and there were four of us? Four of us that were beaten and bruised, tired and still going because we were not disposable. They could no longer throw our lives away as if they were nothing but garbage. Not anymore. I had joined the fight and I wouldn't give until I was dead, or we were free.

Heads surfaced on the stairs as they completed the last steps up, but Rex and Ansel were waiting. They struck fast, not giving them the chance to register the threat before they were falling to their knees, holding their wounds as they sought to live. Did their life flash? Could they remember everything they had done wrong and wished they changed?

Was their last breath thinking of someone they cared for, or did they continue to think only of themselves?

More footsteps fell and above us, glass broke, shattering down through the entrance of the room, falling until it hit the ground in the lobby. The skylight, once the crown jewel of this location, was now used as an entry point as humans corded their way down the opening. To my left, more footsteps. I had forgotten a back stairwell. A simple oversight. We all knew it was there, but it was unused, blocked off for the last five years.

I looked toward Warren, then to Rex and Ansel. The realization hitting us all at once.

We were surrounded, people coming at us from all sides, and if we stood a chance at surviving and freeing ourselves, we would have to do more than fight. We would have to strive. We'd have to be far more superior and wittier. They outnumbered us. They surrounded us. They misjudged us.

And now, we would give them the fight of their life, or we would die trying.

CHAPTER
Twenty-Two

WARREN

Pride.

My chest bubbled with pride as I watched Thea handle the men who came at her. My heart swelled, fighting side by side with Thea and my men. And when Thea protected me, stealing the man who snuck up behind me from the shadows and dragging him into the light, I nearly came on the spot. This girl, she made me so fucking hot just looking at her and the strength and power behind her was unmatched.

Now we were surrounded. People at every side and fuck, I was worried. I couldn't do what I needed to do and keep control if they touched her. They already had once and the roar that left me shook the entire room and I nearly lost control. But again? I might never come back.

The glass that had rained down from the once beautiful skylight crunched under boots as they moved in our direction. We stayed frozen. We could fight, but fuck if we didn't want to at the moment. I was tired, my skin bruised and broken. Chains still clung to me from where they almost got the upper hand. I didn't foresee this going any other way. I didn't foresee us escaping without the death of all on our hands. But hoped to fuck that a minute's rest would be enough for us all to accomplish the goal.

To leave here freely.

Freely. Not in chains. Not in a body bag. To walk out on our own feet and carry our own selves to safety.

The glass crunching under the boots was a stark reminder that we had no control over our lives. Not the humans. Not the mutants. Our lives were in each other's hands and the game we played? It depended on who played it better.

"Get down, hands up." A voice called from behind me, and I didn't look. I didn't dare.

"Fuck off." Ansel lifted his head with pride. "I'd die first."

Thea gasped at his declaration. She had a soft spot for him. Where our relationship was all sharp teeth and quick bites, with him she was different. She was gentle, kind. She wanted to protect him, and I don't know when she would learn that out of the three of us he was the one who never needed the protecting. He could protect himself just fine. It was Rex who would suffer later from all the lives he had taken.

The voice held mirth. "I'll arrange that then."

All at once they struck, bullets flying toward us. Guns, the weakest of weapons. Only used by those who were afraid to get their hands dirty. Didn't they realize that the satisfaction of sinking a blade was much more effective? Feeling the skin and flesh part under the weapon, hearing the crack of bones, brought forth joy that one can't describe unless you experience it yourself.

Without a moment's hesitation, Thea threw a knife. The blade spinning through the air and when it hit her target, it pierced the man's heart, tearing through the protective vest he wore and straight into the flesh. It hit him fast, only giving him time to grunt before his eyes found her and he was gone. Dropped to the ground. Dead.

I lost track of time after that, my body moving forward, trying to clear our path to an exit. My fingers were covered with blood. My hands nicked and sliced from defenses. Guns laid scattered on the ground, broke and bent by my hands and my collection of knives kept growing. Each of them tossed toward Thea, left at her feet like an offering to my own personal goddess. She picked them up without question. Like a skillful marksman, she threw, hitting targets I never noticed until they were on the ground.

The people, the human sacrifices kept coming, the crowd of them thickening. The numbers were vast and fuck, they had to have known. Someone had to have told them we were coming. With over thirty men that laid at our feet and throughout the room, the lobby, the sky dangling with people ready to attack, outnumbered all those that were dead.

Without realizing it, I got distracted. My mind too in awe about the scene in front of me and a chain was thrown my direction. It looped around my neck and pulled me back. Thea screamed, the sound drawing the attention of Rex and Ansel. I strained against the hold of it, dragging the person forward as I stepped into the bit of the chain at my throat. I roared my displeasure, the sound animalistic as it echoed through the building and for a moment every human was frozen. Their eyes were on me as they watched for the next action I would take.

Another chain tossed my direction somehow, looped against my leg, pulling tight on my ankle, nearly bringing me down. I yanked my leg away, tearing the chain out of the grasp of the man holding it. Then I inhaled, sucking hard at the air until his soul parted from his body and floated toward me. I consumed it, letting is slide down my throat without a single swallow and settle in my core as my beast pushed against my skin, demanding I let him out.

I couldn't.

I shouldn't.

Who was to know what would happen if I gave him all the control and released him? It was nearly impossible to take back the reins of my body when that happened.

A body slammed into me. The weight was hardly noticeable as it rode on my back. A sharp pain hit my shoulders, a dagger protruded from my back. I flung my body backward, taking the chain around my neck and using it as a weapon against the aggressor. The metal slammed into his body repeatedly, leaving bloody lashes on his skin before I bent over him, taking the same chain he tried to choke me with and wrapping it around his own neck. The panic in his eyes told me he had expected to win in this situation. But it was too late for him.

Each hand yanked a side of the chain, cutting it into his flesh. His face turned red as he strained against the metal. He was desperate for air, his mouth opened and closed. His lips turned blue and then his eyes glassed over. One more blink and his body went limp. I waited another few seconds before releasing the chains around his neck, pulling it from his body to use as my weapon of choice.

I turned, not hesitating to lash out at the closest person near me, not caring that the force of the chain as it came down on them, powered by the strength I gained from the souls I've consumed, severed his limb from his body. His eyes were wide as instant shock set in. He looked at his arm on the ground, horror on his face before he began to profusely vomit. We didn't have time for the weak stomached. Not when our primary goal was to get out, and that man was standing in the way of any exit we had. Another snap of the chain and his head split open. A cave right down the center was carved through his skull, ending all his movements as he fell to the side.

They were falling fast. Some never fully getting a foot on

the floor from where they hung in the air before Thea's knives took them out, or Rex's pocket of toys decimated them. The ground was red smeared and black puddles. Our bodies covered in so much slickness that every movement was sticky and wet. Thea's face was splattered with blood. Not a single drop of her own and I wished I could take a picture. Enlarge it and frame it to display every day for the rest of my life.

As their people fell as easily as paper dolls blowing in the wind, I couldn't help but wonder what was their objective? If they tore us down, more would sprout up in our place. Did they realize how many people they truly tried to snuff out? How many people they tried to silence that no longer wanted the quiet? As one, we were weak, as four we were strong, but united as thousands, we would be unstoppable.

I watched as Thea blinked in and out. Her body suddenly blending with the background before she appeared at my side. Rex. Had she realized she had taken on a piece of him, moving and blending, so no untrained eye could see? Rex saw her and his back straightened, his chest puffed up, and he looked fucking proud to see our mate honor him in such a way.

Her arm brushed against mine, and my whole body jolted with pinpricks of pleasure. I was aware of her location this whole time, but having her this close, picking a side, right next to me? My chest rumbled with satisfaction. "You do care."

She didn't look at me, but her lips curled into the most seductive smile. "I fucking hate you, Warren."

"Hmm." I hummed with satisfaction. "You said 'I'll fucking hate if you don't fuck me Warren', or am I wrong?"

A tiny laugh escaped before she turned her back, her knives and weapons already concentrated on the men that approached.

CHAPTER
Twenty-Three

THEA

Fuck. Warren.

The audacity of him to ruin my concentration when I needed it most. But I won't deny the fact that having him at my side lent me a little comfort. It felt right that the exact man who dragged me into this mess was next to me fighting it together. He was so fucking infuriating that I couldn't stay away. I was a moth. He was the flame. No matter how hard I tried to pull away, my flight would get stuck in his orbit, absorbing the energy and heat he gave off.

He didn't need a knife. That was my weapon of choice. Whatever his stolen chain didn't break down in a horrific display of strength, his song of souls tore from their body, leaving them limp as their heart stopped beating. There was no escaping it. No matter how they died, it was savage. It was needless. It was a sad truth that only reinforced the division between us all.

The government that I trusted so much, failed me. Failed the humans it employed. Failed us all. They would rather send fifty of their men to their deaths than talk of equality between the existence of beings. It was cruel. I trusted them, and I was only a tool, never their asset.

The worst part? Fucking Warren was right the whole time. I didn't want to believe the government was killing mutants, but it was blatantly clear now. It was painfully clear when they went after me. And well, now I got to watch as familiar faces lunged for me, weapons poised to take my life, giving me no choice but to take theirs first.

My bones ached with pure exhaustion, and this wasn't how it was supposed to go. They weren't supposed to have this many people on hand ready to take us on. Rex and Ansel were only supposed to cause a distraction, maybe take out a single guard or two. But this many? This was planned. The realization was horrifying. The government knew what they were doing when they sent these men in here. They expected their deaths, but hoped one would get us before then.

"Why do they want you so bad?" I grunted as a chain tried to capture around me like I was a hog at a rodeo.

"I have a history." Warren admitted, his chest heaving.

"What type?" What fucking type of history caused all this chaos?

"Let's just say I used to be close with someone high up." A grunt came from Ansel, and my attention swung that way. If anyone hurt that man, I swear I would remove every finger from their hands myself.

He cleared his throat before he spit out blood. Disgusting. But also caused a little worry. Where had he been injured to cause that? "Oval Office."

"What?" I paused what I was doing and turned toward him. The shock overwhelming me. What the hell did that even mean? Warren had connections at the presidential level and yet here we were, at a state level, trying to take over the systems. "Then why are we here?"

He blocked a blade that was aimed at my skull and the

poor soul wielding it had no chance. His soul was snacked on without a second thought from Warren before Warren answered me. "There is information that we need."

"That you can't get at the oval office level?"

He cleared his throat, clearly struggling to keep up with a conversation while in the midst of our own mini epic battle. "If it was that easy, Thea, I wouldn't have to go through this right now, wouldn't you think?"

Hell, I didn't know what to think. I stepped forward, my leg sliding in blood as I skated to the ground, nearly face planting. I righted myself at the last moment. "Clearly that's not what I thought."

Men. Mutants. Males. Menstruation. Membership clubs. Why was anything that started with M so fucking insufferable? If this situation was different, I might have finally finished my fucking mission and drove my knife through his heart. Though I doubted I would ever be able to now. He's grown on me, like a fucking leech that's attached itself to my leg. I can't seem to pull him away without feeling some sort of pain in the process.

A bullet flew toward my neck, and I dodged to the left, avoiding contact. How could I hear that coming? That should have been fucking impossible, right? Regardless, I was thankful. It saved my life. The origin of the bullet came from the other side of the hall, and before the man could get off another shot, Ansel was behind him. He never got to pull the trigger. The gun fell from his hand before he sunk down to his knees, his body falling forward. He landed face first onto a leg of his already deceased teammate and there he laid as Ansel moved onto the next person.

Their people were thinning. The fight more survival now and less brutality. It was no longer killing them off but fighting their strongest assets, hoping to get out of here.

"Put your shadows around you, Thea." Warren growled as he tossed a guy against the wall. He slid down the marble and for a second, I thought he wouldn't get up. But he stumbled to his feet, his head obviously spinning before he charged toward Warren again.

"Why?" I grunted, getting a kick to the thigh.

"These are their best, and you need to be protected."

It was such a man thing to say. "Because I'm a girl?"

"Because you're fucking mine." The declaration rolls out of him without a thought and the sound vibrated through the room. His chest heaved as he tossed the guy around like a rag doll, throwing him back toward the wall. It was nice to see that if he didn't have a weapon, Warren wasn't intent on killing. "You're mine and I need you protected."

"No."

He turned, completely focused on me. "No?"

The man ran and jumped on Warren's back. Warren didn't hesitate to toss him off, this time clearly annoyed. He tossed him over the rail. The sound of screaming echoed through the halls until he hit the ground below. I waited until the screaming stopped to talk. "I'm part of this team."

"No." He growled, his face getting close to mine. "You are the most important thing to the team, not a part of it."

He crashed his lips to mine as someone's life gurgled away from them feet away. Fuck, what was he doing? What the fuck was I doing? I kissed him back, my blood-soaked hands gripping his scalp as I deepened it. His lips pulled away just enough to growl against my own. "I need you to hide in the shadow because you're the fucking most important thing here and if they get ahold of you, I can't control myself. They will want you, Thea. They will want you to get to me."

He bit my lip, and I looked up, his eyes burning into me. The intensity of them sending a shiver down my spine. But I didn't have it in me to just hide. I realized how ironic that was considering my whole adult life. I used my ability to manipulate shadows as my identity to assist and assassinate marks assigned to me. It gifted me the ability to be a success and the stealthiness to get the job done.

But now? There was no mark to get, only lives to defend. Lives of men who, oddly enough, I cared about even though I just met them. I'd never say that out loud, though, at least not to Warren. But what was the point of hiding now when the enemy knows I'm here? When they have known all along that my strength lies in the dark? I could have strength in the light, too. I just needed to prove to Warren that I was an asset and not hindering him.

I released my hand from his hair and forced myself to step back from him. His face was red, both from exhaustion and blood that spattered across his skin. His chest heaved. His eyes flared. Lust filled while he watched me. "I won't hide while you fight."

"Thea." The words came out hard. "I demand that you-"

His demand never finished leaving his mouth. Those fucking chains were back round his throat as multiple men pulled at them, forcing his body away from mine. How the hell had they snuck up on us like that? I hadn't noticed. Of course, maybe if I hadn't used the fact that the enemy's numbers were lightening and then fucking kissed him, I might have known more about what was going on around me.

I lunged forward, but before I could make a move to help him, cold metal hit my throat. The metal dug in, forcing my body backward as another wrapped around my waist. The pull against the chains was strong. The force of people behind them obviously thought I was a stronger being than they were aware of. They effortlessly dragged me backward while the chains on Warren forced him away. His body thrashed as he tried to get free. The sounds that escaped his lips were inhumane.

Glancing to the side, I saw that Ansel and Rex had met the same fate. It hit me then. These men at our feet were knowingly sent to their deaths. They hadn't had a choice in the matter either. The government knew exactly what they were doing. They wanted to wear us down, weakening our defenses because when we were weak, they could get the upper hand. I no longer had the energy I had at the start of the night. I was no longer riding the high I got from having Rex between my thighs. That had all faded and after trying to fight just to get ourselves free? My energy was depleted.

It wouldn't matter if I pulled the shadows now. The chains would still be there, and I couldn't escape that. The voice of Ansel seemed like it was coming to me through a funnel. My coherency jumped. "Fight it, Thea."

But what was there to fight? By all appearances they had won. They had gotten the upper hand, and I didn't see it coming until now. We played into it. We did exactly as they wanted and now? Now we were as good as dead. There wasn't a way out of these chains, not when they were wrapped and twisted around my body and anchored by more humans than was necessary to ensure I didn't move.

I wasn't fucking going anywhere. Not without the men I arrived with.

"Thea, you can fight it." Warren's neck strained as he pulled toward me, dragging the people with him an inch at a time. "You need to get out."

I needed to get out. How the fuck did he expect that to happen? Did he not see we were finally surrounded and weighed down by the weight of metal? I pulled at the chains, they budged slightly, and I used that to move forward toward him. His eyes blazed. I swore the color changed to a blaze of red and orange before settling back to their natural shade.

"Get. Out." His veins bulged as he fought against the hold. "Now."

Smoke filled the air, and I turned my head, looking every direction, trying to find the source. It was seeping in thick, floating around my head and causing people to cough. Only around my head? That was curious. Still, the people coughed and their hold on the chains loosened, allowing me to move forward toward Warren.

"We can get out. The smoke will confuse them." I declared, loud enough only for him to hear me.

He laughed humorlessly at something I hadn't quite understood. "Go."

"I-"

"I cannot, Thea." He was breathing so heavily that the words were nearly impossible to hear. "I can't lose control."

"You don't have to." I wasn't sure what he meant, but I knew he made a conscious decision when he sucked souls. If he didn't have control, he wouldn't have engaged in any of the physical altercations.

"Thea." The minute the warning left his mouth, my body jolted backwards, and an arm went around my throat, holding me tightly against a body.

Every hair on my body stood up as a voice whispered next to my ear. "Your life was never a priority until we saw how much it meant to him."

Him? Why? I felt so damn dense that I didn't understand, but those around me seemed to get it perfectly. Fingers went into my hair, dug into my scalp, and pulled my head backwards. The pain of it caused my eyes to water, but I would not let him know that. "Fuck off."

He laughed as the surrounding smoke thickened. The hand that wasn't in my hair brought a knife up, skimming it across my throat. "The agency hadn't realized just how valuable you were."

"If you're going to do it, fucking do it already." I leaned into the knife, daring him to dig it into my skin.

At the same moment as I dared him to do it, both Rex and Ansel begged him not to. The man heeded no warning from them. "Look at them, not wanting you harmed. Can't they see that they are no longer in control?"

My heart was pounding fast because couldn't he see the same? Warren did not look like he was handling this well, though maybe it had something to do with the overkill of chains he wore. The others, well, they were more controlled but had seen better days. Control was slipping and maybe the guy with the knife held the upper hand, but I knew that it wouldn't last long.

"Fuck you. They don't need control. They are animals, beasts, monsters... or had you forgotten?"

He licked his lips, a drop of spit flying out, and landed against my skin. That tiny mishap made Warren fight so hard against the restraints that he somehow made the chains groan with strain. The action making him laugh. He trailed his knife down my chest before tilting it, so the tip was pressing into the skin. "He doesn't like when I touch you. Curious. So, what happens when my blade pierces your skin?"

Without warning, he applied pressure, the tip nicking the spot between my breasts.

The room went quiet. The sound funneled outward before it was all sucked in. The man hadn't seen it coming and fuck, neither did I. But when Warren lost control, he hadn't been joking about what would come. The chains broke away from his body, snapping one by one like they were mere buttons on an old shirt and not steel meant to be secured. He whipped the chain pieces, taking every single person to the ground with bloody gashes before he turned on them, sucking in such a deep breath that every soul left their bodies at once.

The souls entered Warren's body swiftly. I hardly saw them. When he closed his mouth, he turned his eyes into literal pools of fire as his body grew larger, and skin nearly melted away, leaving only bone in their place. It was terrifying and though I did not fear him in this moment, I was scared. Never in my life had I seen something like this, and I shouldn't be shocked. Not in a world filled with lab created mutants, but I was completely caught off guard.

His bones cracked, making me cringe against the pain I knew he felt as he stepped toward us. His eyes burned into me, practically begging me to help, but I couldn't do shit, not with the man's knife still firmly against my skin. He didn't seem afraid of Warren, though if the roles were reversed, I sure as fuck would have been. Instead, he only taunted him, digging the knife into my skin, and drawing more blood.

Fuck. He was just as insane as Warren.

But it worked. The extra draw of my blood caused Warren to snap, his nose flared and whatever morphing he had been caught between flared to life again, twisting and enlarging his frame, forcing teeth to form out of the skull in front of me as it stretched and moved.

I tried to back up, but the manic laughter and a strong grip held me in place.

"He'll kill you, you know." The man laughed satisfactorily. "But then, we'll take him down. Back to the lab this one goes."

I'd like to believe Warren wouldn't kill me. But I also saw not a single sign of the man I formerly knew in the being that was transforming right in front of my eyes. He was gone and in his place was a complete fucking mystery. I had no clue what Warren had been hiding from me, but I did know that whatever it was, had taken over. Its bones were forming, his eyes were flaring, and with each step Warren took, he changed. Scales traveled up his body, covering the skin as he fell on all fours.

It didn't stop his movement.

His own fire poured out of him and when he inhaled again, the man behind me choked. His body flailed as he clung to me, but the smoke that had once clouded me had attacked. It had gripped the man before it trailed into his mouth and when the smoke pulled free of his throat, his once beating heart was encased in its murky transparency. Like elastic, the black smoke pulled back toward Warren, the heart slammed into his mouth and without hesitation, he swallowed the organ.

It must have triggered something inside of him, or it was always inevitable. The scales and bone finally collided and the man I knew, the sexy and infuriating man, was no longer in front of me. My voice quivered as I tried to speak. It took me multiple tries just to utter his name. But he wasn't there, at least not fully.

He turned his head, focusing on a sound that was mere feet away for a moment, assessing the threat before his eyes met mine. Fire erupted over his whole body, and then...

He charged.

His eyes set on me.

My body urging me forward even as my mind told me to run.

A guttural sound escaped him. One filled with anguish and pain.

I held up a hand, trying to offer comfort. "Warren. Stop. It's me."

But Warren was no longer with me and in his place, towering above me, spanning the length half of the hall that we stood in, was a bone crushing, soul eating, fire manipulating dragon.

And the dragon's rage was set toward me.

Thea's adventure with her men continues in BLAZE.

Like what you read? I would love if you left a review!
Feel like hanging out with me?
Check out my Facebook reader's group, Delilah's Darlings.
Want the latest updates?
Visit me on Facebook at https://www.facebook.com/
delilahmohan/

Website:
Delilahmohan.com
Sign up for my Newsletter here!

-

-

Other works by Delilah Mohan

-

PARANORMAL ROMANCE / REVERSE HAREM
Claiming Claire (A reverse harem shifter novella)
Saving a Succubus
Training A Succubus
Liberty (Keeping Liberty Series)
Justice (Keeping Liberty Series)
Truth (Keeping Liberty Series)
Retribution (Keeping Liberty Series)
Resisted (Wolves of Full Moon Bay book 1)
Refused (Wolves of Full Moon Bay book 2)
Redeemed (Wolves of full moon bay 3)
UMBRA (With the Shadows 1)
BLAZE (With the Shadows 2)
SONDER (With the Shadows 3) Winter '23
Heidi and the Haunters

-

-

CONTEMPORARY ROMANCE
Obscured Love (Obscured Love Series, book 1)
Eluding Fate
Ricochet (Obscured Love Series, book 2)
Five Seconds to Love (Obscured Love Series, book 3)

Resisting Royal (The Repayment Series, book 1)
Owning Emma (The Repayment Series, book 2)
Salvaged Girl
Saints of Sin

Made in the USA
Monee, IL
18 April 2024

56860673R00111